Boy *on a* Tricycle

Boy *on a* Tricycle

DALE HEADLEY

Library of Congress Control Number:		2019906775
ISBN:	Hardcover	978-1-7960-3827-9
	Softcover	978-1-7960-3826-2
	eBook	978-1-7960-3838-5

Print information available on the last page.

Rev. date: 06/06/2019

To order additional copies of this book, contact:
Xlibris
1-888-795-4274
www.Xlibris.com
Orders@Xlibris.com
795963

1

It's not often one's life is profoundly changed by the same person twice - 43 years apart. In my case, it was changed initially in 1950 by Eddie South and his irresistibly gregarious nature, which drew me out of a cocoon of self-centered social isolation. He so completely freed me of my standoffishness that it gave me the courage, in 1953, to go off to fight the commies in North Korea before my draft number was called. And it was a good thing for America that I did because, just as I arrived in Seoul, the war ended. Could have been a coincidence, I suppose, but I prefer to think that the commies gave up when they saw me coming. Sadly, though, I never saw Eddie alive again.

But I guess Eddie's ghost refused to relinquish his hold on me. In 1992, I read in the Los Angeles Times that Chief Constable Edward South of Oak Hill, California - my birthplace - had been killed by a sniper in an ambush at the top of Wolfskill Peak in the southern shadow of the Sierra Nevada Mountains.

So, once again, Eddie had managed to pull me out of my self-imposed isolation following my retirement from the L.A.P.D. I turned off the TV, struggled off the couch, and headed to Oak Hill, where I subsequently solved his murder, and married the love of my life. It may have taken Eddie 43 years to accomplish it, but I finally became a citizen of the world, or at least a semi-rural pocket of it. I was now Eddie's successor as chief constable of my hometown of some 7,000 citizens, a few of whom remembered me from over a half century earlier as that kid who always ran like a demon all over the neighborhood.

I guess about the only thing I don't like about being the Chief

Constable of Oak Hill, California, is speeders. More specifically having to deal with their denials and rudeness. I spend a large part of my time driving up and down the tire-scorching highways surrounding my little corner of the San Joaquin Valley triangulated by Tulare, Visalia, and Porterville watching for people driving too fast. They don't think they're driving too fast, because the traffic is usually light on these rural highways, and their speedometers ease up to 80 mph and above without them even realizing it. It's true enough that traffic accidents out here are not frequent, but when they do occur they are often fatal, due to the speeds involved. Besides, the fines we collect help keep our little town solvent.

And it's not as though I am distracted from the seriousness of my duty by the scenic splendor, because there is none, unless your taste in scenery runs to flat expanses of ground-hugging vegetation in endless shades of dust-shrouded green that slash horizontally across your field of vision. There is the unrivaled spectacle of the Sierra Nevada mountain range, of course, when you can see it off to the east through the brownish-gray plumes of dust kicked up by plows, harvesters, and crop dusters. Otherwise, it's just miles and miles of roads and highways cutting through vast fields of alfalfa, cotton, melons, citrus, grapes, cherries, walnuts, almonds, and tomatoes, just to name a few of the fruits and vegetables that makes this the most agriculturally productive valley in the world. But beautiful? I've never thought so.

As far as water is concerned, most of what at first seem to be rivers and streams are actually aqueducts and irrigation ditches gouged into the earth in order bring water from afar to what is essentially a desert larger than many states. The only natural bodies of water anywhere near my patrol area are the Kern River and Lake Success, both south of my jurisdiction. The most abundant evidence of water comes spraying out of the giant, rotating sprinklers that irrigate the fields. The San Joaquin Valley is a charming, Euclidean patchwork of color if you're flying over it in an airplane, but driving through it gets tiresome pretty fast.

It's also hot much of the year. In the summer it is sweltering. Even so, I almost never use the noisy air conditioning in my car unless

I'm carrying passengers. I prefer the the window down to allow the unfiltered air to circulate, no matter how hot it is.

I don't like hiding my car amongst eucalyptus trees, behind a billboard, or on a side road waiting to ambush speeders. Even without that subterfuge there's no shortage of them for me to bust. These long, straight stretches of highway are an open invitation to speeders, since the traffic is relatively light and the horizons are vast and unobstructed. That means that any drivers who are alert can spot a police car long before their speed can be clocked, and they slow down, which is exactly what I want. I understand some cops, like in L.A. or Frisco, have these new radar guns. So all they have to do is sit under a tree and wait for a car to be zapped by radar before the driver even knows he is being clocked. I suppose I could get the Oak Hill City Council to spring for one of those, but that would take away what little fun I have catching the scofflaws. I prefer to outsmart them, rather than depend on technology to do my job. And one way I outsmart them is with the nondescript car I usually drive: an oxidized red, 1985, Jeep Cherokee.

That day, just a couple of weeks before Christmas, 1993, I was tooling along in pleasant December weather in my aforementioned patrol-car-in-disguise. So as the young lady in the shiny, new, yellow Corvette convertible went flying by me with her long, blonde hair flapping in the breeze, she had no idea I was a cop. At least not until I hit her with lights and siren.

"Ma'am, you were doing eighty five in a fifty five zone."

"That's ridiculous. You're just one of these hick town Barney Fifes who hides behind billboards to extort money from unsuspecting motorists. And it's 'miss,' not 'ma'am.'"

"Miss, I wasn't hiding behind any billboards. You flew by me at high speed, and I was doing fifty."

"Well, I wouldn't have passed you if I'da known you were a cop. What're you doing driving that dirty, beat-up old truck, or whatever it is?"

"The town's only patrol car is in the shop, so I have to drive my own car. Besides, didn't you notice my light bar?"

"Well, yeah, but I just thought it was a fire chief's car or something, being kinda red and all, and you were just goin' to a fire or somethin."

"That doesn't change the fact that you were driving way too fast."

"Hey, come on. There's hardly any traffic out here in the boondocks."

"Maybe so, but see that rise in the road up ahead? This is only a one-lane road each way that keeps going up and down like that for miles, and you usually don't see an approaching car until it reaches the top of the hill. You could suddenly encounter a car coming over the hill a little over the center line, which a lot of the locals sometimes do. If so, you'd stand a good chance of a head-on collision if your mind is wandering at all."

"You're exaggerating."

"Ma'am, in my office I have a photograph of a car where the driver was killed going over that same rise right there. He was slightly over the line when a pick-up truck carrying two-by-fours strapped to the driver's side came from the other direction and they both reached the top simultaneously. He was a little over the line, too, and when their left front fenders met, one of the two-by-fours flew right though the driver's side like it was shot from a cannon and went right through the steering wheel and the other driver's body."

She paled a bit at the picture I had just painted, which is a true story. I still have the photo, which was taken by my father when, as the town's only tow-truck operator, responded to the accident scene over 50 years earlier. I had it taped to the wall behind my desk.

"All right. How much will this cost me?"

"Our policy in Oak Hill is to fine speeders five dollars for every mile over the limit, so that will cost you one hundred and fifty dollars."

"Is that all? Big deal. But I live in Los Angeles. You mean I'll have to drive all the way back to this hick town to pay the fine?"

"No, ma'am. You can mail it in. The information is on the ticket."

Suddenly, she sweetened her demeanor and leaned out of her window to make sure I got a whiff of her perfumed hair and got a look down her cleavage. "How about I just give you three hundred right now and you tear up the ticket? No one needs to know." She reached out and seductively touched the back of my hand, which I instantly withdrew.

"Except that I'll know and it'll keep me awake nights for a month." Here you go. Please slow that 'vette down."

As she drove off, obviously disgruntled, I could tell she was giving me the one-finger salute from behind her door panel. I just smiled, waved, and wished her a Merry Christmas.

Just then, I got a squawk on my radio from my office. It was one of my two deputies. "Yeah, Irma, what's up?"

2

"Arnie, you need to get back to the office. Harry and Bud are here and need to see you."

"Tom's deputies? Did they say what they wanted?"

"Yes, but I'd better let them tell you."

This was my first day back from a vacation in Yosemite National Park, a few easterly miles from Oak Hill, with my wife, Marjorie, and my recently adopted 11 year old daughter, Nancy. I wondered what was so urgent that two of Tulare County Sheriff Tom Whiting's deputies were paying me a visit all the way from the county seat in Visalia.

Being a lazy sort who avoids responsibility, I was really getting to like being the Chief Constable of Oak Hill. My name is Arnie Crockett, by the way. True enough, I've had a couple of harrowing and exciting adventures since I came here almost a year ago to find out who killed my best friend. I had been an L.A.P.D. detective and had retired to a cabin in the mountains of Southern California in order to leave all that stress and responsibility behind. And it was working quite well until I read in the L.A. Times that my former best friend, whom I hadn't seen in over 40 years, had been murdered. That got me out of my blessed torpor and I took the 300 mile trip to my birthplace to help find out who had shot and killed Eddie at the top of Wolfskill Peak, east of town. It only took me six days to do that - six very hectic and exciting days. Not long after that - after I had been coerced into taking over Eddie's job - I found myself solving the murders of two local teachers; that, too, proved to be pretty stimulating.

But, by and large, being chief constable here in Oak Hill has been pretty darned uneventful, which is the way I like it. I also like working with Duane Altmeier and Irma Kamimura, a pair of energetic, smart, young deputies. Duane, who resembles Jimmy Stewart in Destry Rides Again, minus the cowboy hat, also happens to be the son of my wife, eighth grade crush, and love-of-my-life, Marjorie. And, although he technically moved out of his mother's house when we got married, he pretty much still lives with us, not wishing to give up his mother's extraordinary cooking legerdemain.

Irma is a third generation Japanese-American - a Sansei - and absolutely indispensable at keeping the Oak Hill constabulary humming efficiently. Efficiency is not a defining feature of either Duane or me. Basically, I'm a procrastinator and Duane's in love, though not with cute, adorable, little Irma.

My family consists of Marjorie, and my new daughter, Nancy, 11, but almost 12, whom we adopted after rescuing her from the compound of an insane killer and his henchmen. Nancy is extremely bright, but mostly uneducated, though we are trying to make up for that as fast as we can. And I don't want to leave out Kojak, my German shepherd mix who's getting along in years after being pretty much my sole companion when I secluded myself in my mountain retreat after I retired. Not since the arrest and conviction of the teachers' murderer had much of anything happened in this little town, which, as I said, is just the way I like it. But I guess nothing stays the same forever.

As soon as I entered the lobby of the police station, diminutive Irma, positioned behind the counter minus her usual bright smile, was dealing with a local farmer I recognized as a frequent complainer about local kids annoying his pigs. She looked up blankly, pointed towards my office, and quickly lowered her head to the task at hand. I knew something was wrong. When I entered my office, there were Harry Benoit, sitting behind my desk, and Bud Markus, standing and staring pensively out the window towards Wolfskill Peak to the east, now blanketed with snow in anticipation of Christmas coming up in a couple of weeks. Both of them were in their mid-40's and very competent, experienced detectives in the Tulare County Sheriff's Department. The sheriff, himself, was not with them. I took a quick glance around to make sure, since I rarely saw these two without Tom. But not this time.

Bud turned away from the Ansel Adams view in the window and came over, unsmiling, to shake my hand, then he slumped down in the only other chair, leaving me standing. Bud tended to be less than loquacious. Just now, he was even more subdued than usual, which is saying a lot.

"Hey, good to see you guys. How's it going?"

"Not too bad, considering."

"Considering what, Harry?"

"You didn't know?"

"Know what?"

"Tom's been killed."

"What? NO! Tom Whiting? When? How?"

"He was shot to death in his home last Monday night; it was in all the papers and on TV."

"No Harry, I didn't know. Marjorie, Nancy, and I just got back last night from a week long camping trip, and we had no contact with civilization. I overslept this morning and didn't get a chance to look at the paper or turn on the TV. How..."

"Shot in his own home."

"Do you know who did it?"

"No, no idea. At least not yet. Look Arnie, here's the murder book we're working on." He pointed to a standard murder book on my desk. "We could sure use your help." Bud leaned his gangly body forward and placed his elbows on my desk with his acne-scarred face obscured by his clasped fists. He seemed to be fighting back tears.

"Fucking wrong, man."

"Absolutely. That's the worst news, ever." I stood there, stunned, not knowing what else to say. Tom Whiting was the Tulare County Sheriff I'd met the first day I came to Oak Hill, and he'd since become a very close friend - someone I could work closely with on tough cases. He was even on national TV in connection with the capture of the anti-government nutcase, Esau Reinart. It was hard to believe he wouldn't be around anymore, with his 300 lb. bulk and his deep, commanding baritone. If there was anyone who appeared indestructible, it was Tom. Just goes to show.

Harry Benoit was Tom's #1 detective, an intense, serious professional with wispy, black hair swept back over his head, and an equally dark, heavy mustache. His sartorial choices were uniquely his own. The upper half of his body was pure detective: brown, tweed sport jacket, pale blue button down shirt, and a tan clip-on tie. His lower half was all cowboy: well-worn jeans with the legs tucked into shiny, snake-skin cowboy boots. On special occasions, he added a fedora, which gave him a kind of aura like Gary Cooper in The Fountainhead. Meanwhile, his partner, Bud, resembled Cooper in his "Yup" manner of drawling speech, but looked more like Buster Keaton.

Harry wasted no time flipping open the murder book and getting down to business.

"Jeez, Harry, I can't believe that Tom's gone. How did it happen?"

"I don't know where to start. It all began with that." He pointed at the murder book. I glanced at it and noticed the name on it was not Tom's.

"This says Violet Strand."

"That's right. We haven't opened a murder book on Tom, yet. This is the case Tom was working on when he got shot."

"Tom didn't usually handle many cases himself solo, did he?"

"No, not usually, and that's why I think this is connected somehow. He was really wrapped up in this one."

"How so?"

"Well, I hate to say it, but Bud and I busted our butts to solve the murder of this Strand woman but got nowhere; and I mean NOWHERE. So Tom decided to take it over, himself, and right away he seemed obsessed."

"So you think his murder had something to do with this one?"

"We're pretty sure it does, because his murder and this Strand one have certain characteristics that strongly link them to another one."

"Another one?"

"Yeah, some guy named Walter Knobb in Visalia, who was killed a month earlier."

"Why would that link it with Tom's murder?"

"Because all the same unusual characteristics were present with Tom's killing, so we assume Tom was killed for what he was learning in the other two cases."

"Did he write anything in this book that gives you any clues?"

"Not that we can tell, other than the M.O. similarities. My guess is that he was killed over something he found out that he hadn't yet had time to write down."

"Wow. How can I help?"

"Well, the thing is that we haven't been able to come up with one iota of evidence or any kind of trail to follow; as I said, we don't even have enough to open a murder book on Tom, yet. There was virtually no forensic evidence of any value left at any of the three killings, and nothing in the backgrounds of the victims suggest any of the usual directions to follow. Miz Strand was the second one killed, and she was single - and had no relatives, at least not in California. She had no friends that we know of - a really private woman who stayed home when she wasn't working. She was around 56, married just once, nor could we find any ex-boyfriends in her past. She had no financial issues we could turn up. And the neighbors have nothing but nice things to say about her. In short, we have nowhere to go with this one. We thought we could concentrate on the Knobb murder and you could take over this one and see if you can spot anything we missed."

"By 'this one', you mean Tom's murder?"

"And maybe Strand's, as well. We have some leads in Knobb's case."

"So, you haven't any clue about the motives?"

"No, but they all suggest that someone wanted very badly to kill these specific victims, execution-style, with one bullet to the head. This Knobb guy has a bit more of a sketchy background, but we were only just getting started on him when Tom took over. Tom always said you had kind of a sixth sense, especially when it came to motives, and that your "jigsaw puzzle" technique always seems to come up with a motive nobody ever thought of, so..."

"First of all, it's not MY technique. It's something I learned from John St. John - you know, 'Jigsaw John,' when I worked with him in L.A. But hey, you know I'll do everything in my power to help you find out who killed Tom. Where would you like me to start?"

"We thought that we'd leave that up to you."

"How about we take a look at the murder scene?"

"Or murder scenes, plural."

"Right. Let me study this murder book, tonight, and I'll meet you guys at your office, tomorrow morning. 9:00?

"Perfect."

That's at your main office in Visalia, right?"

"Right." That Bud - a regular chatterbox.

The Tulare County Sheriff's Department has three offices - one in Porterville, one in Tulare, and the main one in Visalia. My little police station, located in a residential neighborhood in Oak Hill, was about equidistant from each - about a three mile drive to any of them. I took Highway 63 north.

Back about the time I was in elementary school, I would occasionally ride with my father when he had business in Visalia as a volunteer Oak Hill deputy constable. At that time it was a hot, dusty, two-lane road running through alfalfa fields. And that hadn't substantially changed, until I crossed under the Visalia Parkway bridge, and it became a modern highway lined with businesses on both sides fronting miles of densely-packed, single family homes that appeared to have been built in the 70's or thereabouts. I noticed that quite a few homes had swimming pools. That was virtually unheard of when I was a kid in the 40's. For that matter, nobody even had air-conditioning back then. The only way to survive the oppressive heat was with swamp coolers. Air conditioning as we know it was invented about the time I entered my teens, but it took longer than that for them to reach our part of the world. I mostly remembered my birthplace as being hot all the time. Being the middle of December now, though, the temperature was pleasant enough.

I was also surprised when I reached the sheriff's office. Where it had once been a dinky, little structure like the one I now occupy, it was now a large, modern, semi-circular, convex, two-story building constructed almost entirely of mottled, red brick and large, reflective, glass panels.

I took an elevator to the second floor. When I lived in Oak Hill, an elevator was something we only saw in movies. A two-story building was essentially the town skyscraper. I entered Harry's spacious office, with pale green walls covered with framed photos and certificates pertaining to Tulare law enforcement officers, past and present. Harry and Bud were ensconced comfortably in upholstered, brown leather chairs poring over documents and evidence boxes laid out on a large, circular table, covered in brown formica in the center of the room. I waved at them briefly as I checked out all the photos, hoping my father might be among them. But, being just a small town volunteer constable, like myself, he wasn't.

3

I was eager to get started. Not only did I want to get justice for my friend, but I could stop handing out speeding tickets for a while. So the three of us drove in their cruiser to Violet Strand's home nearby. It was a two-bedroom, tan, Spanish-style stucco - neat, clean, and unpretentious. It was surrounded by a 4' chain link fence. Nothing about it implied wealth or ostentation. It was unoccupied, and the tattered crime scene tape was still tied to the small trees in the yard. We entered with a key. The inside was just as mundane as the outside. Harry and Bud had already removed anything of possible evidentiary value, all of which had fit inside a 7 1/2 cubic foot cardboard box, not exactly a treasure trove of forensic evidence. So we were looking at the house essentially unchanged from when the murder occurred.

The first thing the detectives pointed out was the perfectly circular hole, about 8" in diameter, cut out of the glass patio door right next to the lock mechanism. Sand-like deposits of crushed glass remained in tiny piles beneath the hole on the outside, with an unbroken glass circle lying on a welcome mat on the inside. It appeared that the glass had been etched with something sharp - deep enough that it could be punched out with relative ease. It was unusual enough as an M.O. that it strongly linked the murders, even though forensics had yet to compare the bullets at all three murders. Not surprisingly, no fingerprints were left around the hole; so either he wore gloves, or he took the time to carefully wipe off fingerprints or other trace evidence. In either case, the intruder was very meticulous, it appeared.

Both detectives pointed up the straight staircase.

"That's where she got it - her bedroom,", said Harry.

"Yup."

We took a look through the house for anything out of the ordinary that might have been left after the cops, detectives, and forensics people had carted away anything of apparent evidentiary value. But we found nothing unusual other than the hole in the glass. So we sat down on the immaculate, cloth, flower-print couch and reviewed what I had learned from her murder book as prepared by my friend, Tom.

Violet Strand's financial records showed that she had accumulated a fairly substantial nest egg by saving it in small amounts over many years. And her bank book suggested that she rarely withdrew any large sums of money. There was nothing in those records to indicate any sources of income other than her librarian's pension and her wage working part time as a clerk at a flower shop. She had no investments in stocks, bonds, or annuities; or at least nothing that had turned up, so far. There were no indications in her records that suggested a safe deposit box; but that would be double checked at her single bank of record. If she had any substantial amounts of cash stashed somewhere, it wasn't reflected in this house or in the aging, grey, compact car sitting forlornly in the driveway.

There was no sign whatsoever of a sexual assault, or any other kind of physical confrontation. She had been found in bed, seemingly asleep, with nothing to immediately suggest she was deceased, except for the hole in her head behind her right ear made by a .22 caliber slug. There was no exit would, so very little blood. She probably died instantly and painlessly - just the way I would choose to go. It appeared that the killer had gained access in the middle of the night by cutting a circular hole in the glass door just big enough to be able to reach inside to unlock it. He then crept up the stairs, entered Violet's bedroom, apparently unnoticed by her, and placed his gun no more than an inch or two from her head, judging by the powder stippling pattern, before calmly pulling the trigger. There was nothing to suggest rage or personal passion. It was methodical, as far as they could tell. It had all the earmarks of a well-planned, professional hit, except that Violet Strand had nothing in her past, as far as Harry and Bud knew, to suggest that she would be anyone's target for assassination. Still, that was what it looked like.

A burglary gone wrong was a possibility, but Detectives Benoit and Markus said that, since no drawers and cabinets had been found open, there was no way of knowing if anything had been stolen, because no one knew what it was she owned that was worth stealing. Besides, the items in all the drawers and cabinets showed no signs of having been disturbed, and there was some money in a purse on the dressing table. The TV appeared untouched and there was no sign that she had ever owned a computer. If jewelry was taken, it was not evident; no jewelry box, for instance, and no stray pieces that are usually left behind by thieves in a hurry. And someone who had just committed a murder is likely to be in a hurry. Also, everyone who knew her said she never wore jewelry and doubted she owned any. Cash might have been taken, but, if so, how much? Judging from the evidence of her bank book and monthly bank statements, it is doubtful that she kept much loose cash around. There was no personal lawyer revealed in the scant amount of paperwork found. There was no indication amongst her bank records of either a life insurance policy or a will. We all three concluded that there had to be some connection between Ms. Strand and the Chief, not to mention the third victim. A canvass of the neighborhood had produced no one who had heard the shot or saw anyone fleeing the scene.

The killer left no trace evidence of any kind. No fingerprints; no shell casings; no blood; no new-fangled DNA; no hairs; no footprints. The sound of the shot may have been muffled by something, since no neighbors remembered hearing anything. But the sound of a .22 is not very loud. A silencer is a possibility, but silencers are mostly an artifact of fiction; real murders are rarely committed with guns with silencers. They are not sold at Wal-Mart. The stippling around the wound was heavy, so the closeness might have muffled the sound of the shot, especially if it was a contact wound. The absence of any casing implied that it was likely a revolver. Automatics usually kick out the casing to the right and often for some distance. Most killers don't have the presence of mind after hearing the explosion of the shot, to crawl around looking for a hot casing in a dark room, assuming this took place at night, which is likely since Ms. Strand was shot in bed, seemingly while asleep. They just get the hell out. And most people with semiautomatics have 9 millimeters or .45's, not .22's.

"Any estimate yet of time of death guys?"

"Probably sometime the night before she was discovered," said Harry. "No more precise than that, though." The temperature wasn't hot, though, so the M.E. should be able to narrow down the T.O.D. with reasonable accuracy.

When I went to bed that night, I thought hard about all of this. Before drifting off to sleep, I made plans to visit Tom's murder scene forthwith.

4

The first thing I did the next morning before leaving for Tulare, where Harry and Bud were working that day, was take another quick look through Violet Strand's murder book. She had no relatives living west of the Mississippi. Her parents were deceased. She had one sibling - a younger sister named Audrey Jackson, living in Nashville. I did my due diligence and called her. She didn't seem particularly grief-stricken. She had been informed by Harry of the death of her sister, but she was unable to contribute anything at all about Violet that detectives didn't already know. The sisters exchanged Christmas and birthday cards, and occasionally they spoke on the phone, but they had not seen each other for 35 years. Just to cover all the bases I could, I asked Ms. Jackson whether there was anything in the way of assets involving Violet that she knew about. There was nothing, she said, but she did inquire about whether Violet had left anything. I told her that, as far as I had been able to determine, she left neither a will nor any substantial property. That pretty much terminated the conversation.

Being obsessively punctual, I showed up at Tom's former Tulare office right on time to find Harry and Bud huddled around a smallish, scratched-up, rectangular oak table that looked older than I am, and was well-used. They were sifting through all the evidence, such as it was, in the murder of the first victim, in Tulare, Walter Knobb. I dropped the Strand murder book on the desk.

"You were sure right about nothing to go on", I said. "The only thing interesting about this book is what's NOT in it, but should be. No forensics or any other physical evidence, other than the twenty-two slug in her brain, which almost certainly came from a revolver, and the tight-pattern powder stippling above her ear. No personal or business associations to track down. No history of anything but a pretty boring life. No friends or relatives listed, except for the sister in Nashville. I called her this morning and she was no help at all. Man, I can see where you guys might have been tempted to call in a psychic.

"We did."

"You did what?"

"We called in a psychic. That's you, Arnie."

"Very funny, Harry. That being said, I usually have at least something in my own past that helps me pick a path - some intuition - to follow. With Eddie's murder, I already knew people of whom I was a bit suspicious from the old days, just on general principles. With the murders of the teachers, my experience with religious kooks gave me an inkling of what the motivation might be. But this one? Absolutely nothing in my experience gives me any direction to take. What've you guys learned in the murder of whatsisname..."

"Walter Knobb."

"Yeah, Knobb."

"Well there was one interesting thing," said Harry, "The home was furnished with cheesy furniture, like Ikea and 1930's, upholstered furniture. The paintings and photos on the walls were generic and cheap, also. But I noticed two places where there had obviously been some framed items removed, and they were nowhere to be found on the premises.".

"And you would think that if Mister Knobb had taken them down himself, he would have immediately replaced them, wouldn't you?"

"I would have," said Bud.

"That does look suspicious doesn't it? Whaddya wanta bet that a picture of the killer used to hang right there in those spots?"

"Wouldn't surprise me," Harry agreed.

"I don't suppose anybody thought to search trash cans and dumpsters in the neighborhood."

"Of course we did,"

"We sure did."

"And?"

"Nada," said Bud.

"Do you really think anyone who planned these murders so carefully would make a mistake like that? Especially if it was a professional hit?"

"Hey, Harry, he might if he had reason to believe that small town detectives wouldn't think of it."

Harry didn't say anything, but he gave me an unhappy stare.

"Cheap shot," said Bud.

"Yeah, you're right, sorry. None of us is Sherlock Holmes, or even Columbo. We make mistakes. Anyhow, I'd bet that, whoever this killer is, he wouldn't have been so slipshod. Fortunately, even the most careful killers do make their own mistakes. We'll find one. For example: my guess is that those photos or whatever they are that were hanging on that wall currently reside on property to which the killer has access. He might have destroyed them, of course, but, in my experience, these guys can't help keeping some kind of souvenir. Because, sick as they are, they're often proud of what they did, and like to keep reminders around. Back in L.A., it always amazed me that, whenever we caught a killer who used a gun, he almost always still had that weapon on his person or at his home, instead of getting rid of it. They just can't help it. Well, enough speculation; how about we visit the murder scene where Tom was killed? I know where he lived, so how about I give you guys a ride, this time?"

"In that old Jeep without the air conditioning you never use?"

"Hey, Harry, I'll run it, just for you, if you don't mind the noise it makes."

"Why not?"

Tom had lived in a middle class community of what song writer Malvina Reynolds called "ticky-tacky little boxes", less than a mile northwest of this Tulare Police Station; but we drove there in Harry's cruiser, once my A.C. rattled his brains. The modest, neat house was located in a tract of nearly identical two-bedroom homes built in the early 70's. Harry, Bud, and I all ducked under the crossed bands of crime scene tape and entered Tom's empty house using a key. Tom had been a widower whose wife had been killed in a car crash while he was in the police academy. He lived alone, though his girlfriend, Laura, was there a lot.

"Okay, guys, what do we know about what happened?"

Harry answered, as usual. "Best as we can tell, it happened somewhere between eight and ten P.M., last Monday night."

"How did the killer get in?"

"That's the only thing we know for sure; he came in right over here."

They led me to the sliding glass doors to the patio.

"He used a glass cutter, just like in the other murders." said Harry, as Bud pointed to a circular hole in the glass, about five inches in diameter, adjacent to the inside door handle. I carefully stuck my small fist through it. It immediately occurred to me that the killer was probably on the small side, as well. At least he had a small hand, it appeared. "A perfect circle. So he must have had one of those doohickies with a diamond cutter on the end of a cord and attached to a suction cup."

"Looks like it. I guess he just made a circular cut, knocked the class out and reached in to unlock the door.

"Do you have the circle of glass?"

"Nope, the perp evidently took it with him, this time."

"Weird. So, forensics doesn't have it?"

"Uh uh." Bud doesn't waste words.

"Uh, uh,' Harry confirmed, "but they do have them from the other murders."

"The killer entered this way in all three murders?"

"Looks like it."

"So what is it about this one that made him take the time to take away the glass?"

"Good question."

"I'd say he didn't want forensics looking at it. It takes a pretty cool customer to take time to cut out the glass, commit the murder, then take the glass with him. If I had to guess, I'd say he cut himself and couldn't take time to completely clean off the glass."

"Could be. In any case, this guy's very meticulous," said Harry.

"And yet he wasn't quite that meticulous, to use your fancy word, at the first two murders if he left the glass behind; why so careful with this one? Blood?"

"I know that the big police departments are starting to get pretty good at identifying someone by looking at their blood through microscopes. Got something to do with genes or chromosomes or something"

"So where was Tom's body found?"

"Right over there." Bud pointed to a spot about 10' away - halfway between the front door and the apparent point of entry, next to a small wet bar.

"Not asleep in bed like the other two. How was Tom dressed?"

"Casually, with a robe, but not yet in his pajamas. It looks like he was in the kitchen, since there was a cocktail shaker and a glass on the counter, with both half full."

"Okay, I'm not getting a coherent picture here. Are you saying that, while this guy was busy cutting a hole in the glass, Tom just stood here watching?"

"No, that makes no sense. So maybe he was in the kitchen or something, then came out here and ran into the guy with the gun."

"And he either hadn't heard the guy cutting the glass or he responded to the intrusion without his own gun? Tom? What kind of gun was he shot with?"

"The slug is a .22, just like with the other two. I'm sure that forensics will establish that it was the same gun."

"No doubt. How close was he shot?"

"Within three feet, judging by the spread of the powder burn pattern, but not close enough to cause heavy stippling."

"So the killer broke in, managed to get within three feet of Tom, who was about three hundred pounds and always kept a gun nearby, and shot him without leaving any signs of a struggle?"

"That's sure the way it looks."

"Where exactly did he get it?"

"In the back of the head."

"Okay, so now you're saying Tom came in, saw the intruder, then turned around so the guy could shoot him in the back of the head? Or are you saying that Tom was just standing here in the middle of the room with his back to the glass doors as this guy was cutting though it?"

"Doesn't make sense, does it? Maybe Tom heard the guy breaking in, came out to see what was going on, and ran into the guy with the gun, who pointed it at him and made him turn around before he shot him."

"Possible, I guess. But it seems to me, Harry, that if Tom heard something suspicious he would have armed himself before checking it out."

"But if he did, maybe the killer took Tom's gun away from him," said Bud.

"Really?"

"Well, not likely," said Harry. I found Tom's service pistol right where he always kept it, over there in that little desk in the hallway. So he either didn't grab it, of the killer took time to put it back in the drawer"

"That assumes he knew where Tom kept his gun."

"Not likely", said Bud."

"And if he did," said Harry, "it would have to be someone Tom knew awfully well."

"But if that's the case, what was his motive for killing the other two. Very strange. Something doesn't track, here. Any fingerprints, blood, anything like that?"

"Nothing except a small pool of blood right there." Harry pointed to a spot on the hardwood floor where there was still a small stain of blood. It suggested that Tom died instantly before he could bleed out. Thank goodness for that."

"And no footprints outside? Not even any depressions in the fresh grass?"

"Nope"

"Really, Bud? Could he have gotten onto the patio without crossing grass or dirt? Harry?"

"It doesn't appear so. He must have climbed over the fence along the alley."

"Climbed the fence? But Harry, that fence is about six feet high. If he dropped over, he would have landed in that soft dirt. And you're saying there were no signs of footprints there?"

"Not a one."

"So, it appears that some perp climbed over that fence, which he would have had to do to get into the yard, but he managed to land inside without hitting the dirt and leaving some kind of impression? Tom grew flowers along his fence; that dirt would almost certainly be soft."

"I dunno, maybe he smoothed out his footprints after he landed."

"Maybe. If it was me, though, I would have simply worn oversized shoes or boots and not worried about leaving footprints, inside or out. Were there any signs of footprints on the patio cement?"

"No, none there, either."

"Not even a little dirt he might have tracked in?

"The patio cement was clean as a whistle."

"None of these explanations make any sense."

"Hey, Arnie, that's what you're here for. If you can think of an explanation, we're all ears."

"So, apparently this killer simply floated over the fence and landed on the patio with clean dry shoes."

"Unless you've got a better idea."

"I might. Tell me, were any shards of glass found?"

"Yeah, I don't know if I'd call them shards, but when Bud and I got here there was a tiny pile - dusting, really - of crushed pieces of glass lying by the door, just like at the Strand killing."

"Inside or outside?"

"Inside, I think, wasn't it, Bud?"

"Yeah, mostly inside."

What about at the other murders? Were the same kinds of shards piled by the door?"

"Yeah."

"And were they found inside or outside?"

Harry and Bud looked at each other and said, together, "Outside."

"Now that you mention it," said Harry, "the glass fragments in those other two killings were outside. I see what you're getting at; you'd think the glass fragments would be lying outside the door in this killing, too, wouldn't you?"

"Most of them, anyway, if he cut the glass from the outside and punched it out. But if he did that, you'd think the glass circles would have been broken, and they weren't, if forensics has them intact. And they were intact, right?"

"Right" Bud contributed.

"We need to get crime scene techs back here to see if they can tell for sure if this hole was cut from the inside or the outside. But why would the glass have been cut from the inside at this scene but outside at the others? For that matter, why'd he cut it from the inside at all?"

"You have an idea about that?"

I might, Harry, but let's talk to your forensics guys, first. Was the door locked when cops arrived?"

"Yeah."

"What about the alarm system? Tom told me once that he had a state of the art security system put in."

"It was turned off when the cops got here."

"So the Sheriff of Tulare County, who spent a fortune on an alarm system, didn't bother to use it?"

"Maybe he only turned it on when he went to bed."

"Maybe, but if it was me, I'd have it on all the time. I also keep the doors locked, even when I'm home, and only turn the alarm off for invited visitors. Tom was raised in the projects in South Philly; I would expect him to be in the habit of locking his doors as soon as he came in the house. Like I do."

"Where'd you live?"

"Mostly South Central Los Angeles."

"I see what you mean."

"Actually, in my case, it's just one of the many idiosyncrasies

I've developed over the years. I also wash my hands at least a dozen times a day."

"So, whaddya think, Arnie, your jigsaw puzzle coming up with anything?"

"Maybe. I've already got a dozen pieces that do seem to fit into one possible theory, but it's too soon to go off half cocked in that direction without a few more pieces that fit the puzzle."

"So, you have any wild guesses you'd like to entertain us with?"

"Well, I'm thinking that Tom's killer did not come in through the glass doors. I think Tom let him in, completely unaware that he was about to get shot by someone he didn't regard as dangerous. I think he recognized the visitor or visitors, turned off the alarm, and let them in, then was shot almost immediately."

"'Or 'visitors,' plural?"

"Maybe, but I doubt it. If there was more than one, it increases the likelihood that Tom wouldn't have let them in. I'm pretty sure this was only one shooter. After the killing, he took time to make it appear as if he'd broken in by cutting that hole in the glass. I have no clue why he would do that, though, except to obscure the fact that he knew Tom well. Anyway, when he was finished, he unlocked the patio doors and left the house through the front door, which he took care to lock - very thorough. Incidentally, who reported the killing?"

"When Tom didn't show up for work, it set off alarm bells in his office. So it was some of our own patrol guys who found his body."

"But not you two?"

"Naw, we were at the Knobb murder site at the time."

"What I don't get," said Bud, suddenly becoming downright chatty, "is why he took the glass with him."

"Good question, Bud. Maybe the blood, like I said before. Also, if I put myself in his place, I might be concerned that forensics experts looking at it could tell it had been cut from the inside, and it was important to him that investigators not realize that he was someone Tom knew and trusted."

"Then why didn't he sweep up the crushed glass on the inside?"

"Another good question. Perhaps something interrupted him and he didn't have time to get something to scoop up all the pieces and put them outside. Maybe he thought us hick cops wouldn't notice. Heck, maybe he just forgot. It's rare that even the most careful killers don't make some kind of slip."

"Why didn't he do the same thing at the other two murders where he left the glass circles behind?"

"Hell, Harry, I don't know. Maybe it was because he wasn't known to those victims, and his motivation for killing them was too obscure for him to be concerned about leaving that kind of evidence behind. He figured there was no way in the world the victims could be connected to him. Unfortunately, that means that it's going to be that much harder for us to know where to start. I think the other killings were planned well in advance. At the first two murders, he probably did break in with his glass cutter, but this time, he knew Tom had a good alarm system, which also suggests some familiarity between them. But Tom's murder was a quick, necessary decision that he didn't have time to plan that carefully. He figured that, by making it look like it was a break-in, it would throw us off as far as looking for someone Tom knew. Not many serial killers are that painstaking in their planning, so I could be wrong; but it's a piece that fits into the puzzle I'm starting to put together in my head. But, at this point, the final, big picture is pretty foggy. The job now is to start clearing it up."

"Any ideas where you want to go next."

"How about going back to the Strand murder scene?"

"Again? Why?"

"Well, now that I've seen Tom's house and yard, I want to re-examine Strand's for comparisons"

"I got nothing better to do," said Harry.

5

Violet Strand's home was enclosed by a 4 foot white, chain-link fence. The inside was best described as spartan. No ostentation or any other indication of wealth. The furniture was plain and functional. The walls were mostly bare, with a few photos and tasteful paintings. And I noticed that there were no missing spaces on the wall, as there were at Walter Knobb's murder scene. That suggested to me that the killer was not as intimately acquainted with Ms. Strand as with Mr. Knobb. Maybe. Harry said the photos were of her long-deceased husband, and an as yet unidentified younger woman who might or might not have been herself in younger days. No children were evident.

I took a closer look at the hole cut in the glass door. Like the others, it was perfectly circular. However, this one was a bit larger - maybe 8" in diameter - than the one at Tom's house. I pointed that out to the detectives. That reinforced the notion that it was cut with a diamond cutter on the end of a string attached to the glass with a suction cup, rather than a commercial glass cutter.

"Did you notice that, before?

"No, not me. You, Bud?

"Uh uh."

"You think that means something?"

"Maybe not. But what it suggests to me is that this one was cut large enough to easily fit his hand through. But at Tom's house, he cut it in a hurry without any concern about the size, since that wasn't his point of entry. Just one more hint that Tom knew his killer

"Interesting."

"I noticed that you guys never mentioned anything about what the neighbors have had to say."

"Well, we canvassed the whole block, as well as the side of the street behind the house, and zippo. Everyone was asleep when it happened and don't recall hearing any noises like a gunshot. Same at the other two murder scenes. So they all probably happened late at night. And nobody recalls having seen any suspicious people or vehicles in the neighborhood."

We did a thorough inspection of the rest of the house, but it didn't take long, because there wasn't anything remarkable about it, and anything of possible interest had already been carted away to the sheriff's department. The back yard yielded nothing of interest. If any footprints had been left, the killer had taken time to obliterate them.

Just as with the other two murder scenes, evidence was sparse to non-existent, so we didn't remain long. On the way back to the station, I said, "Well, Harry, I want to start, like we always do, by talking to the people who knew Tom best. Usually, we start with family, but Tom didn't have any family that I know of. The connection is likely to be elsewhere than in Tom's family. In any case, this killer is very intelligent, a cool customer, and very ingenious in his planning. My guess: this is going to be tough to solve. For one thing, a lot of these killings are solved when the killer goes to a bar, gets drunk, and lets something slip. Or maybe he spills his guts to somebody he mistakenly thinks would keep his secret. But I'm pretty sure this guy is never going to make that kind of careless mistake, especially after all the careful planning he's done so far. Even if we assume Tom knew his killer, that still leaves a huge suspect pool; a sheriff makes lots of enemies. My gut feeling, though, is that this killer is someone with whom Tom had never crossed paths before this investigation, and yet someone he never actually suspected. I'll have to remember to keep that in mind, because I'll almost certainly run into this guy, myself, at some point. The key to solving Tom's murder is to find the link between the murders of Miz Strand and the other guy..."

"Walter Knobb"

"Knobb, yeah, funny name. The motive for their murders must

have some connection to why Tom was killed. We may not yet have a good idea of the motive for his murder, but if we find out what links the other two, that might give us the motive we need. But my own suspicion is that Tom was killed because of what he was finding in his investigation of the other two murders."

"You know who you want to talk to first?"

"I do - Laura Duval."

"Tom's girl friend? Why her? Serial killers are nearly always men."

"True, and this one's probably male, and I don't think for a second that Laura had anything to do with this, but Laura's been with Tom for a long time, and if anybody knows what his innermost thoughts might have been about the cases he was investigating, it would be her."

"Me and Bud already talked to her, but she said that he said hardly anything about it."

"Nothing at all?"

"Well, nothing we didn't already know already."

"Still, I might be able to think of some questions to ask her that you overlooked, like we all do. I know that every time I finished interviewing a witness I wanted to kick myself for forgetting to ask some question. And you know the old saying: three heads are better than two."

"Oh, THAT old saying."

6

Laura Duval lived in one of the newer homes off the main drag of Visalia. It was a low-slung, faux ranch-style with an attached garage, shake roof, and a small but neatly landscaped front yard. As I knocked on Laura Duval's door, I was thankful that I wasn't the one to have to bring her the awful news. Laura was white, born and raised comfortably in a nice part of Philadelphia. Tom was as black as they come, brought to the U.S. from Jamaica as an infant and raised across the tracks, so to speak, from Laura. He had endured wrenching poverty and senseless racism as a child. They had met when he was a Philadelphia street cop who investigated an attempted jacking of her car. Later he made detective and earned such a brilliant reputation that he was approached by Tulare County to take over a troubled department. Two people were never so seemingly mismatched, but they didn't notice; they were in love. They hadn't yet married, partly because they hadn't decided whether or not it would be wise to have children, especially given the problems that come with being mixed race. But they were so serious about each other that, when Tom was hired as chief in Tulare, Laura moved to California to be near him. She'd had time to deal with the grief; so, when she opened the door, nothing on her face showed any kind of emotion. Aside from the fact that she was a very nice, smart woman, it was no mystery why Tom had fallen in love with her.

Laura was tall - 5'9" - and delicately slender - a sleek beauty - with long, thick, black hair, slightly waved. Her complexion was clear and smooth. She had expressive brown eyes, full lips, and a perfectly sculpted nose. If she was wearing any make-up, I couldn't tell. But then, what I know about women you could put in a thimble and it would rattle around like a B-B in a boxcar. I think I heard that on an old Red Skelton TV show.

"Oh, Hi, Arnie, come on in." She displayed no outward emotion other than the weakness of her smile.

As soon as I stepped inside and she had closed the door, I said,

"First of all, Laura, I want to apologize for not being at the funeral. Marjorie and Nancy and I were off camping all week. I didn't know about this until yesterday."

"That's okay. To tell you the truth, I was so distraught at the funeral that I hardly knew who was there and who wasn't. That was probably just as well, because some of the people there had no idea Tom was with a white girl. That would have raised some eyebrows, i suspect."

"Is there anything I can do? Anything you need?"

"Thanks, Arnie. Nothing."

"For what it's worth, I was devastated by the news. Hit me like a ton of bricks. Tom was my idea of the perfect lawman - smart, thorough, fair, tough, and decisive. Furthermore, he was unusually kind for a cop. And for what it's worth, he could hardly stop telling me how much he loved you."

"Thanks, Arnie, I appreciate that. He was quite impressed with you, as well."

"Couldn't ask for greater praise than that. If you're up to it, I thought maybe you could answer some questions I have."

"I hope I have some answers."

I breathed a sigh of relief. "Can we sit down?"

"Of course. That chair's comfortable." I accepted her offer and she sat at the end of the large couch as I leaned forward, up close, so I could talk in low tones. I guessed it had been Tom's favorite easy chair, judging by the deep depression, suggesting that somebody weighing 300 pounds had spent some time in it.

"I understand from Harry and Bud that you weren't home, that night."

"No, I was visiting friends in Porterville. I gave the detectives their names."

"Well, just so you know, none of us think you could possibly be involved in Tom's murder. You are not only NOT a suspect, you are not even a person of interest. They also told me that you said Tom had never discussed what he was investigating with you."

"No. He usually did, but he had only just got started on this Strand murder and hadn't learned anything yet worth talking about. You think his murder had something to do with it?"

"That would be my guess. The main thing I wanted to know, since you would seem to be the one who would know best: did Tom keep his alarm system armed, even when he was home?"

"Absolutely. The first thing he did when anybody came calling was to turn off the alarm; and the first thing he did when they left was turn it back on. He was obsessive about it. He said he hadn't felt the need of one till he started planning for me to move in."

"So I'm guessing he was the same way about locking his doors and windows."

"Pretty much, yeah. Is that important?"

"Very much so. It means that there were only two ways for the killer to get in: he either cut through the glass of the patio doors, or Tom let him in."

"Harry said that he broke in through the patio."

"Maybe. But now that we've taken a closer look, that seems more and more unlikely. As soon as the forensics guys take a good look at the glass hole cut in the doors, my guess is that they will realize it was cut from the inside."

"Are you saying you think whoever killed Tom was somebody he let into the house; someone he knew and trusted?"

"That's what I think, yeah. Not only that, but somebody who took the time to make it look like he was a stranger who broke in."

"I hope you aren't including me as one of those people he mistakenly trusted."

"Oh, I'm sorry if I gave you that impression. No, Laura, absolutely not. Like I told you before, we are certain you had no involvement.

There were two other people killed in exactly the same way before Tom. Unless you've been a serial killer all this time and I didn't know it."

"Not funny, Arnie."

"You're right. I'm sorry."

"That's okay. Is there any other way I can help you?"

"Well, I don't mean to beat a dead horse, but can you think of anything Tom might have mentioned, even offhand, that would give me some idea of what Tom was thinking about these murders. I know that I share everything with Marjorie."

"Well, Tom was like that with me, too, but he kept saying that this was the toughest case he'd ever had - that he couldn't find anything, either physical evidence or possible motives. He said that Miz Strand and Mister Knobb were both boring people who lived boring lives and other than a little pot dealing by Knobb, were not involved in anything illegal or suspicious that he could find. If he had, he would have told me, I'm sure."

"Did he have any other cases he was working on?"

"I don't think so. If he did he didn't tell me."

"Yeah, I'm almost sure he was killed by somebody connected to those other two murders. Did he mention the names of any people he talked to during his investigation?"

"No, sorry. I don't recall him mentioning any names."

"Too bad; my guess is that whoever killed him was somebody he ran into while investigating the other murders. I don't suppose he kept any notes about his investigation here, somewhere."

"No, he never brought his paper work here. I really wish I knew something that would help, but I just don't."

"Well, I don't want to take up any more of your time, Laura; I know you must be having a tough time and probably don't need me making it tougher."

"Hey, Arnie, come anytime. And Marjorie and that cute little Nancy, too - even Kojak." Kojak was the German shepherd I brought from California. The previous year, he had saved Nancy's life when a hired killer broke into our house.

"Right back atcha. When you're feeling up to it, Marjorie would love to have you over for dinner. She's a helluva good cook."

"I know she is. Give me some time, then please invite me again."

"You can count on it."

As I was headed for the door,

"Arnie, I just thought of something. It's probably nothing, but..."

"Hey, Laura any little thing."

"Well, The day before he...the day before, he casually mentioned something about having to check with Arizona - Phoenix, I think."

7

Tom Whiting, being the sheriff of Tulare County, had a secretary. Her name is Arlene, and it was to her I headed as soon as I got back to the sheriff's office. She was in her mid-40's and quite pale and thin, Tom's direct opposite. She was clearly distraught and haggard, and I could see she had been crying. I had no intention of questioning her any more than necessary. Harry and Bud had pretty thoroughly taken care of that necessity. I pulled a chair up next to her desk and waited for her to collect her thoughts before asking her, "Arlene, do you know if Tom got any calls from Phoenix in the last week or two?"

"Not that I can recall; but let me check the phone log."

She got out a spiral notebook from her upper right hand drawer and thumbed though it.

"No, he didn't."

"Could he have called Phoenix without going through you?"

"He could have, yes, but if he did, he didn't tell me, or log it in."

I sat and thought about that, for a bit. Tom had mentioned Phoenix to Laura, so he must have had it on his mind. It was a long shot, but what did I have to lose? With Arlene's permission, I used her phone to call the Phoenix Police Department. She had it in a Rolodex at the upper right hand corner of her desk. That's when I noticed she had no computer that I could see - old school. When I called, I was a bit surprised to get an automated response that asked me to select which department I wanted. As soon as I heard "Homicide, three," I pushed the number 3 on the phone.

"Homicide, Lieutenant Martinez."

"Yes. Lieutenant, my name is Arnie Crockett, the chief constable of Oak Hill, California; but right now I'm calling on behalf of Tulare County, I..."

"Tulare? Where Chief Whiting was killed?"

"You know about that?"

"Of course, Sheriff Whiting was famous around here; he was on the "Today" show a few months ago talking about that big bust of the people who murdered those teachers."

"Yeah, that was Tom."

"Did you say your name was Arnie Crockett?"

"Right."

"As I recall, Sheriff Whiting spent most of his interview on the show talking about you. That was you, right?"

"I vaguely remember something like that."

"What can we do for you, chief?"

"I have reason to believe that Tom was concerned about there maybe being some connection between your department and a couple of murders he was investigating here."

"Hold on, chief, I've got another detective here who might be of more help to you."

I waited almost three minutes.

"You're calling about Sheriff Whiting?"

"That's right."

"And you are..."

I had to go all through it again.

"Okay, chief, here's what I know, so far. I'm Sergeant Morrissey, by the way. I called Sheriff Whiting's office about a week ago to ask him about the murders there in Tulare County. I'd read about them in the Arizona Republic. I didn't talk to him, though. I left a message with another detective to have Whiting get back to me; but I guess he was killed before he could return the call."

"Really? Our local murders rated newspaper space all the way over in Arizona?"

"Well, you know, that murder case where the teachers were poisoned made the national news, and Sheriff Whiting made quite an impression on the "Today" show, which I happened to watch. And what struck me was that these two recent murders Sheriff Whiting was investigating there were exactly like one we had here, recently."

"How so?"

"Well, to begin with, it was the hole cut in the patio window; that's pretty unusual. Then there is the fact that the killing was done with a single gunshot to the head of someone sleeping."

"Interesting. By the way, chief, what was the caliber of the slugs in your murders?"

".32 - a revolver, probably."

"Too bad. The murders here were done with a .22. But the hole in the patio door..."

Sergeant Morrissey and I agreed to immediately exchange faxes with all the information we had, so far. By the time we hung up, it was getting late - time for me to get home. But I knew I couldn't sleep, so I took home Walter Knobb's murder book to study it carefully. I tend to think more clearly when I'm horizontal; or when I'm running; I figure it has something to do with getting more blood to my brain. So, after dinner with Marjorie, Nancy, and Duane, I kicked back on my couch and started reading.

Mr. Knobb, like Ms. Strand, and me, was pretty much a reclusive homebody. Unlike Ms. Strand, though, he did have some relatives, friends, and possible enemies to be tracked down. He seemed to be earning his living through some kind of phone business, which needed to be looked at pretty closely. In terms of evidence from the scene, the book read exactly like Violet Strand's. Someone broke in through the sliding glass doors late at night, crept to the victim's bedroom, and executed him with a single shot to the head. He left nothing behind. A lack of fingerprints suggested gloves. A lack of fiber evidence or body hairs suggested the killer was covered with something that left no fibers - something like a hooded raincoat, perhaps. No footprints were even hinted at, so he might have gone so far as to put something over his shoes. This was all wild speculation, of course, but the bottom line? The killer was very, very careful about leaving any possible trace of having been there at all; except for the victim, of course. I was afraid that whatever evidence might exist somewhere, it wouldn't be found at the murder scenes.

8

Right after checking through Walter Knobb's murder book, which was virtually identical to Violet Strand's, in terms of the way the murder was executed, and in the evidence left - or not left - at the scene, I went to bed and opened Violet Strand's murder book once again, largely to compare it with Knobb's.

Violet, born Violet Strand (She reverted to her maiden name after her divorce) in 1937, was 56 years old when she died on October 11, 1993. That makes three victims, all essentially the same advanced age; that doesn't happen often, so I decided to treat it as significant. The owner of a local florist shop had called the police headquarters in Tulare to report that one of her employees, Violet Strand, had not shown up for work. She said she was scrupulously punctual, but she had not been able to get her on the phone. Tulare cops told her that they couldn't investigate a missing adult for 48 hours. But the shop owner was so distraught and insistent, that they called the Visalia P.D., where Violet lived, and that department agreed to send a patrol car to her house to check on her, since it was only a few blocks away from their station. When the patrolman got there, he noticed a car was in the driveway, but no one answered the door. So he went around back and immediately spotted the hole in the glass. He considered that to be an exigent circumstance that would allow him to enter the house without a warrant. The sliding glass doors were unlocked, so he slid them open and called inside for Ms. Strand, but received no response. So he walked in and looked around on the bottom floor, noticing nothing askew. Then he went upstairs, where he found Violet deceased in her bed, with a gunshot wound to the head, very little blood, and no sign of a struggle.

Violet Strand had been born in Visalia and lived in this one house all her life. She had only been married once, very briefly. The ex-husband was contacted, but quickly eliminated as a suspect, having been working in Alaska at the time. She had once been the town librarian, but had retired 3 years before her death. Her neighbors described her as very quiet, but pleasant whenever they encountered her gardening. She rarely left the house except to go to work or buy groceries. Currently, she worked part time in a florist shop seven miles away in Tulare. As far as anyone knew, she had no boy friends, or close friends of any kind; at least none that the neighbors ever saw.

9

The next morning when I got to my office, I looked over the fax sent from the Phoenix P.D. Besides the coincidence of the hole in the glass, there were other similarities with how the killings in Tulare County had been executed. The Phoenix victim, too, had been shot in the head while sleeping. The victim was a male - 57 years old - named Gordon Prospero, and he was found dead in his bed in an upscale home in nearby Scottsdale. Both the Scottsdale Police and the Phoenix Police were working on the killing. The close similarity of his age with that of Ms. Strand hadn't registered very strongly, at first, but then I remembered that Mister Knobb, the second victim, was also 57. It's one thing for a string of victims to be in the same age category, but all within one year of each other? I didn't know how significant that was, not yet, but an experienced detective doesn't ignore coincidences like that.

Now that I knew the ages at death of all three, coincidence was becoming evidence. Then I realized, when I looked at the date of the Phoenix killing - October 22 - that, if the Phoenix killing turned out to have been linked to the local murders, Mister Knobb's would have been the third, not the second, since he was killed on November 10. And Ms. Strand's was the first of the three, October 11. Tom's murder, on December 3rd, broke the pattern, because, for one thing, Tom was a good ten years younger than the other victims. He was also the only one not killed as he slept. And it was the only scene where the glass circle was carted away. All of this suggested to me the probability that, while the others were probably premeditated, Tom's was more likely a spur of the moment decision. Were it not for the ballistics match of the slugs, Tom's murder might not have even been considered connected to the others. It further suggested a personal motive of some kind for the other three victims, but fear of exposure in Tom's case. At least that's what made the most sense to me. Four victims, SO FAR. And just as I was considering the chances of the ages being a coincidence, which I thought unlikely, the age issue became all the more relevant. It turned out that the victim in the Phoenix murder - Gordon Prospero - who was the same age as the others in California, was born in Visalia. And the fact that they all had once lived in Visalia at the same time, told me I was on the right track. That was too much coincidence to be coincidence. These three murders were not only committed by the same person, but the motive likely went back to when Mister Prospero last lived in Visalia. When I looked through the murder book more thoroughly, I finally found it: he left Visalia in 1955, at about age 18, and never returned. All I could think was "WOW!" In their early teens, all three victims had lived in this small town, though one had left at around 18. So everything was telling me that the motive for this murder could well be something that happened between the victims and their future killer before 1955. Now THAT'S unusual! And there was little doubt in my mind that, at one time, they had all known each other. That meant that either someone had been carrying around a profoundly deep hatred for around 40 years, or they had all been involved together in some way that reverberated, even today - economically, culturally, politically, even criminally - with something so important that someone felt the need to kill these people. Hard to believe, but I could think of no other explanation that fit all I had learned, so far. So how hard would it be for me to find out who these four people were back in the day and what exactly had been their connection? There HAD to be one, I was pretty sure. But, as it turned out, it would be very hard to determine. The good news was that I wasn't dealing with a random serial killer. Some of them operate for years without being caught, because nothing connected the victims. This case was different There would be evidence to be found, sooner rather than later, I was sure

What all this did for my investigation was cause me to put the usual motives - money and sex - on the back burner for now and start plugging pieces into my jigsaw puzzle with a rough picture in mind of a decidedly unorthodox motive. Three teenagers had been living in the same small town - probably with their eventual killer, who was probably a teenager also, otherwise, he'd be very old by now; and most killers are not more than about forty or fifty years old. Of course, the killer could be someone older related to one of the victims or to someone they knew. But somehow, my gut told me otherwise. If that had been the case, what would the motive have been for killing the two who were not related to the killer? I sensed that my jigsaw puzzle lacked that key piece - the one that provides the puzzle-solver with his "AHA, NOW I see it!" moment.

Then another thought hit me: is this killer done? Were there only these three people against whom he had carried around a bucketful of vengeance or retribution all these years? or were there others, yet to be murdered? That put a lot more urgency into my investigation.

What did I know for sure? Except for Tom, who was probably killed because he was closing in on the killer, all the people had been murdered in an identical and unusual manner. And they were all about the same age, born in the same small town, but only two were murdered there. The third was evidently tracked down in another state by the killer, hundreds of miles away; and shot with a gun of a different caliber. Two of them lived all their lives in Visalia; but one of them, Mister Prospero, had left town at the age of about 18. The only conclusion I could come to was that the motive was linked to something that occurred before Prospero left town, 38 years ago. The next thing to try to determine was what connection, if any, there was between these three people, all young adults in Visalia up until 1955, that caused such intense hatred to simmer in the heart of someone for so long.

First, I had to make sure what connection Gordon Prospero, who had lived in Phoenix all these years, had in common with the ones still living in Visalia. I sent a fax to Phoenix, describing what I had and what my theory was. That didn't help. They faxed back that, since I was already on scene where I thought this whole murder scheme was hatched, and since the murderer was almost certainly in my immediate vicinity, I should take the lead and keep them informed. In other words, they passed the buck.

10

As soon as I got to Tom's office, Harry and Bud were already there. Both of them looked beat. Harry's tie was loose and his jacket looked slept-in. Bud was was down to his tee shirt, and his thinning hair was sprouting at all angles. They had clearly been drinking a lot of coffee, but I was thankful neither of them smoked. I can't stand to be near people who smoke. Bud was reaching over to pull a cardboard evidence box over between them, and I joined them.

"What's up, guys?"

"Good morning chief sleepyhead; it's about time you got to work. Coffee?"

"Thanks. Never drink it. Can't even stand the smell of it. Hey, Harry, it's exactly nine o'clock, official starting time. And besides, I don't live down the street like you guys; I have to come all the way from Oak Hill."

"You could stay at my place until this case is solved, if you want."

"No way, Bud; I have a wonderful wife and daughter waiting at home for me every night. Besides, Marjorie is a helluva lot better cook than you."

"Can't argue with that."

Harry interrupted. "We were just starting to open the evidence box from the Strand murder scene and take another look to make a point-by-point comparison between these two cases."

"Is the other one Tom's?"

"Nah, forensics is still working with that one. This is that guy Walter Whatsisname's..."

"Knobb," inserted Bud.

"Knobb, yeah; you'd think I'd remember a name like that. Anyway, we decided to go over Strand's first; dig in."

We started pulling out items from the box, one-at-a-time.

"Are you guys just getting around to looking at this stuff?"

"Well, we turned it over to the forensics lab as soon as we got it; then Tom took over. So, even though I collected the evidence from the Strand murder, and Bud collected it from Knobb's, we've really never had a chance to look it over carefully and compare them, ourselves, till now.

We started pulling out one seemingly innocuous item after another: a hairbrush, a small photo, a magnifying glass, a paperback novel, a pencil, an empty coffee cup, even a paper clip.

"Not a lot of stuff, here," I noted unnecessarily.

"Nah, this lady kept her place obsessively clean. This stuff is all from her night stand, as I recall. Since she was obviously killed in her bed, Tom didn't think that anything other than a cursory look all through the house would be productive, at this stage."

"Probably not."

"But if we come up empty on everything else, we might have to go back and go over that house with a fine tooth comb; maybe find a motive."

Bud hadn't said much; but he was obviously concentrating hard on this meager pile of evidence. "Hey, wait a minute!"

"What's up?" said Harry.

"I just thought of something." Bud reached over to the other box from the Knobb scene, and opened it.

"Hey pard, we're not done with this one, yet."

"Yeah, but..." He pulled over the Knobb evidence box and opened it. "Yeah, here it is!"

He pulled out a small photograph. "Look at that. I knew I'd seen it somewhere before. It was on Knobb's nightstand."

I looked at it and realized right away that it was an exact copy of the one we had just seen in the Strand box. "I'll be damned!"

"And I'll join you, chief; let me see that." Harry grabbed it and stared back and forth between the two photos. All three of us looked like we were watching a tennis match. There were no two ways about it: these were two identical copies of the same photo of a small, grinning boy sitting proudly astride his tricycle.

"You said this one was from Knobb's nightstand?"

"That's right, Arnie. right in the middle. Just a minute...here it is." He removed a crime scene photo and, sure enough, this photo had been right in the middle of the nightstand. And when we checked the Strand box, another photo showed the same placement of the photo.

"That CAN'T be a coincidence," I said.

"Not in MY book," said Harry, "What do you think it means?"

I thought it could only mean one thing, but I didn't say anything, yet.

"Are these the forensic notes?"

I was looking at an 8 1/2" x 11", typewritten list of the items in the box. After each one was an indication of what trace evidence and/or fingerprints were found. Trace evidence? None. Fingerprints, plenty - all belonging to Violet Strand. Her fingerprints were found on all of the items that would take prints - all except the photograph; there were no fingerprints of any description anywhere on it. We looked in the Knobb evidence list and found the same thing: lots of fingerprints of people who had been identified and cleared, but none whatsoever on the photo.

"Okay, guys, tell me, why are there no fingerprints on these photos?"

"Come to think of it," said Harry, "that makes no sense."

"That's right. Of all the things here, the thing that would most likely retain a fingerprint is this slick photo. Think about this: who put this photograph on Strand's nightstand?"

"Violet?"

"Then why, Harry, didn't she leave her prints anywhere on it?"

"Gloves?"

"Yeah, right. And was she wearing gloves when she was found?"

"Sure wasn't; and there weren't any gloves lying around any place."

"Well, there you go. It would be nearly impossible for that photo to be on the nightstand unless it was put there either by Violet or her killer. If Violet had put it there, there would almost certainly be fingerprints; unless, of course, she was wearing gloves, set the photo on the nightstand, then put the gloves somewhere else in the house, which makes absolutely no sense. I'm assuming you didn't find gloves in her bedroom."

"Sure didn't," said Harry.

"The only logical explanation is that the killer put it there after wiping off his own prints. Furthermore, he did the same thing at Knobb's murder scene."

"And why would he do that?"

"Well, Harry, I think it's because he didn't want us to know who put it there."

"No, I mean why did he put it there in the first place?"

"I think he wanted to send it to Hell with his victims so they would know what crime they were paying for."

"A revenge crime."

"I'd lay odds on it, Harry."

"So who do you think this kid might be?"

"I have no idea; but I can tell you this: he's not a kid anymore. First of all, these are old - very old. It's not just that they are black and white, though. See these ripples around the edge of this one? And 'KODAK' on the back?"

"Yeah," said both Harry and Bud, simultaneously.

"When I was a kid, I was a real camera bug. I took snapshots of everything I could think of with my Brownie. Along about the late forties and early fifties, Kodak started developing the photos and putting them in these little mini-albums, about four inches square. You could either leave them in the album or tear them out. This one has rippled edges where it was torn out of the album."

"But the other one has smooth edges," said Bud.

"I'd say this rippled photo is a good forty years old, maybe older. A better question might be why there are two of them. They didn't routinely print duplicates except by special order. That may have been done when they were first developed, or maybe later but I'm betting, in this case, this smooth one wasn't copied from the negative, but from the print. And if I'm not mistaken, it was done fairly recently just so it could be left at the scene. And if you look closely," I overlapped the two photos, "they are not exactly the same size - close, but no cigar. This one was printed at least 40 years ago, and I'm betting this one was made just recently, just so it could be left at the scene. I don't suppose there was one like it at Tom's murder...Harry?"

"No, there wasn't."

"I didn't think so. Knobb and Strand were killed for personal reasons - probably reasons that go way back; but Tom was killed out of sudden necessity. The killer had no reason to send him to Hell with a reminder. One more thing: this rippled photo looks as fresh and new as when it was developed, forty or fifty years ago. Someone has taken great care to preserve it. I think there's someone out there who has been carrying a hatred for our two victims here and the one in Phoenix for a very long time, since he was a kid, probably. We might be looking at our killer right here. The question is: are there more victims to come? The next thing to do is call Phoenix P.D. to see if they had a photo like this with their vic. I'll bet ten dollars they did."

"No bet," said Bud.

"I'll take care of that. For now, I want to just sit here awhile thinking about what this photo might tell us. I'm sure it fits into my jigsaw puzzle; I just have to figure out where." As far as I was concerned, THIS was my "AHA!" moment - my key piece of the puzzle.

11

After Harry and Bud went home, I used their phone to call Phoenix P.D. Sergeant Morrissey informed me that, in fact, there WAS a small photograph of a kid on a tricycle alongside the victim; they had just assumed it was a relative of Mr. Prospero that just happened to be lying around. Although I knew the answer, I asked, "Were any fingerprints found on it?"

"Just a minute...as a matter of fact, there weren't."

That left no question whatsoever in my mind: everything centered on identifying this kid, perhaps our murderer.

"Sergeant, be sure to take good care of that photo. If I have anything to say about it, it'll end up in court some day,"

So I hung up, then sat staring at the photo. It was a little boy, about 4 or 5, sitting triumphantly on his tricycle. I wondered if I really was looking at the killer, or some kind of victim. I couldn't discern a brand name for the tricycle. Nor was there anything about the clothes the kid was wearing that would aid in identification, no logo on his white tee shirt, for example; but they did look dated. There was a house behind him, likely his own; but there was nothing distinctive about it that might help locate it today, fifty years or so, later. The house was similar to many others in the region a generation ago, including the one I grew up in: a plain, single story gray, clapboard with a small porch in front. In the upper right hand corner, I could see in the background over a rooftop, the top of some kind of business establishment - a gas station, I thought - about 200 yards away, but I couldn't identify it. I had a good magnifying glass in my desk, so I took it out and studied the photo intently like Sherlock

Holmes. It turned out that the distant structure was indeed what we used to call in those days, "a filling station." This one was a "Flying 'A'" station. If I could somehow determine where this now probably defunct station had been located, all those years ago, it might help me locate the house in front of which the boy sat, blissfully unaware of his profound place in the scheme of things in the universe.

12

I thought I remembered that gas station from when I was a kid, and I thought I remembered where it had been located, because my father had hung a picture of himself standing in front of it at his towing garage business. I have a pretty good memory for such things. I even remembered my father wiping his hands with an oil rag in the photo.

So, on a whim, I drove over to that neighborhood and found a parking place in the general vicinity of where I thought the kid's photo might have been taken. I got out and walked around for a while before deciding it was a tiring and likely futile effort, since all of the houses were at least two decades newer than the one in the photo. So I decided to shift gears, so to speak, and do some wider investigating sitting comfortably in my cop car.

It occurred to me that one person I hadn't yet questioned was the lady who ran the florist shop where Violet Strand was briefly employed. And, as far as I knew, Harry, Bud, and Tom hadn't interviewed her, either. So, leaving no stone unturned...

I didn't hold out much hope of gaining much information from this lady, but it was worth a try. Besides, a good detective leaves NOTHING to luck. The biggest breaks often come from the most unlikely sources.

When I got to the "Promises Floral Emporium," about a mile north of the police station on "M" Street, I entered, causing a little bell over the door to tinkle. A neatly attired, middle-aged lady came out from a back room. She was about 5'2", with silver-streaked black hair cut short and tightly-curled; she was wearing bifocals with pink plastic rims. She wore a similarly pink, flowered, house dress. I guessed her age as early 50's.

"What can I do for you? Oh, I see you're a policeman, aren't you?"

"Yes ma'am; I'm Chief Constable Crockett from over in Oak Hill."

"Your kind of far from home, aren't you, young man? That's what, eight miles from here?"

"About that. Thanks for the 'young man', especially since I'm pretty sure I'm older than you."

She offered no response to that. "Is this business or pleasure?"

"Business - MY business, anyway."

"How can I help you?"

"I understand you're the one who called into the station that Violet Strand was missing."

"Poor Vi, that's right."

"911?"

"No, I didn't want to alarm a 911 operator if it wasn't necessary. They might think I was a hysterical old lady, or something. Violet was only a couple of hours late. But that wasn't like her; she was very punctual, so I just called the Tulare police and they connected me to the Visalia Police Station. I had to argue with them for a bit, but they finally decided, since it was close by, that they would make a quick check to see if she was all right."

"And she wasn't."

"No, she certainly wasn't."

"I was hoping you might be able to fill in some of the details about just who Miz Strand was; what she was like."

"Well, she was about my age, maybe a bit older. She was very quiet, sweet and serious."

"She never mentioned any kind of problems with anyone?"

"No, never."

"How did she get along with customers?"

"Wonderfully. Actually I wouldn't normally hire anyone her age, but she said she needed the money, so I decided to give her a try, and she didn't disappoint me; she was great, especially with the older customers."

"Had you advertised for help?"

"No. She just came in one day and asked for the job. She sounded kind of desperate, and it was hard to turn her down."

"Really? She came all the way here from Visalia to find a job?"

"She said she needed it badly, and she said she knew a lot about flowers and gardening, but there weren't any flower shops in Visalia that needed help."

One thing I knew about Violet Strand was that she had plenty of money to be able to live her simple lifestyle. Why would she be desperate for more money?

"Do you know if she had already been looking for other jobs?"

"No, I don't, except for whatever flower shops she tried in Visalia."

"So you didn't already know her?"

"No. I know Visalia's a small town and everybody there knows everybody else; but she was a very private, reclusive, person; hardly anybody knew her."

"And yet she was driven to go out and look for a job at her age. Something doesn't fit."

"I know what you mean. But I can't help you a lot, because, even though she worked here, we seldom chatted."

"One more thing." I pulled out my photograph, which I figured I would be showing to a lot of other people. "Would you by any chance recognize the child in this photograph?"

"She took it in both hands and studied it carefully. "I'm afraid not." She gave it back to me, without further comment.

"Well, thank you very much, Miz..."

"Missus. Missus Myron Linderman. My first name is Alice."

"Missus Linderman. Thanks again."

Just as I was tinkling my way out the door, Mrs. Linderman said, "Wait a minute. I just remembered something."

I turned around and stepped back inside.

"I just remembered that Violet did mention once that she was kind of worried about some Asian man who was always walking past her house at all hours."

"Thank you, I'll sure check into that.." I wondered how come none of the neighbors mentioned seeing such a person

13

When I came into their office the next morning, Harry and Bud had resumed going through the evidence boxes; but now they also had Tom's.

"Come up with anything, guys?"

"Not yet," Bud mumbled

"Hey, let me ask you this. Didn't you guys say you canvassed the area around the Strand murder scene?"

"Of course," said Harry, "I walked for about two blocks on one side of the street and Bud took the other side."

"Nothing?

"Nada."

"Did anybody happen to mention a strange Asian man hanging around the neighborhood before the murder?"

"Nobody I talked to said anything like that. You, Bud"

"Nah, me neither. Why're you asking?"

"The lady at the flower shop said that Violet had mentioned someone like that walking near her house."

"Interesting, but none of the neighbors mentioned it. There's lots of Japanese folks in this area."

"Hmmm. Well, here's what I'd like to do. While you guys concentrate on these two vics, I'll keep in contact with the detectives in Phoenix. Also, I have some ideas about that photograph of the kid on his tricycle. This guy, Walter Knobb may provide you guys some avenues to investigate, since he had no shortage of friends, relatives, and maybe even enemies to interview. Personally, I suspect that's a dry hole, but we can't dismiss it; we have to investigate it. So, if you two don't mind, I'd like to have you follow leads in that direction while I try to figure out who this kid was and how he fits into all this.

"Fine with me. You, Bud?"

"Me, too."

"Okay, Arnie, you take that half of the office and we'll take this half."

"Thanks, guys."

While Harry and Bud rummaged through items spread out on the table, and concentrated on possible leads to follow in Knobb's murder and Tom's, I moved to a small desk in the corner and just stared at my little photograph until I'd worked out a plan. It didn't take long to come to the conclusion that my best bet would be to try to determine the location of the photograph, which was clearly near a "Flying 'A'" gas station 50 years ago or so, possibly the one in my father's photograph.

The first thing I did was drive over to the Visalia Public Library and conduct some research on "Flying A". The Associated Oil Company, originally operated in the late 19th century as a subsidiary of Tidewater Oil in New York, and it was a very popular brand, especially in California. In 1966 it was acquired by Phillips Petroleum, and they still exist; today, though not in the numbers they once did. Although there were a lot of these stations in California in the 50's, Visalia was a pretty small town, then, and I suspected that there was only one here at the time, and I was looking at it in the photograph. I thought about what might be the best way to determine for certain where it had been.

Since I was in the library, I used its microfiche viewer to scan old copies of newspapers for a photo, but found nothing. Neither did the library have any old archival photographs that showed a gas station. Next, I thought maybe I could contact the company to see if they had archives they could reference, but figured that would be difficult, so I decided to leave it as a last resort. Then I thought of the local newspaper, the Visalia Times Delta; they might have old issues I could look through. On my way back to Oak Hill, I took a detour and headed over to the newspaper office, I happened to pass the City Hall. So, just for the heck of it, I thought I'd stop and see it they had archival photographs. To my astonishment and delight, as I walked into the building there was a long hallway with old time photographs lining the walls on either side. I walked slowly down the hallway and came to a large black & white, sepia-toned photo of downtown Visalia in 1950, according to the brass plate at the bottom, and it prominently featured a "Flying A" gas station. I took out my little photo of the tricycle boy with the top of a gas station in the background and looked back and forth between the two till I had satisfied myself that they were one and the same. I tried to make out the names of the streets in the large photo, but couldn't. The nearest office was that of the City Council, so I went in there and spoke to a secretary. She called for a couple of other employees, including a janitor, to help me. It was the janitor, a gentleman of around 60, who recognized the station's location, with the help of some other now-defunct business establishments, like the Woolworth Department Store, in the same large photo.

"Yeah," he said, "That station was on the corner of Noble and Conyer Street."

"Was that the only "Flying A" station in town?"

"As near as I can recall, yeah."

"Are there homes near that location, now?"

"Matter of fact, some pretty nice ones. Not so nice back in the 50's, but solid middle class, today."

I was disappointed with that bit of news. it meant that the house in my little photo almost certainly no longer existed. Still, there was a chance that somebody in the immediate neighborhood of where the picture was taken might have lived there for many years, and would remember this kid. So I set out to find out why cops are called "flatfeet."

I drove to the corner of Noble and Conyer, which happened to be just across the 198 freeway from Redwood High School. The thought struck me that all of our victims, and possibly their killer, might have attended that high school; but I put that aside, for the time being. The north side of the freeway was mostly business establishments, while

the south side, where I was now slowly driving, was all residences.
The janitor had told me that the station had been on the southeast
corner and faced west. Today, there was no gas station, but there was
a sizable apartment building. So what I did was drive around the
neighborhood until the building appeared to be at about the same
distance and direction as the gas station in the photo, so I pulled over
to the curb and parked. The only thing left - the hard part - was to
start walking and knocking on doors. That's the unglamorous part
of police work you don't see much in the movies and on TV.

I would estimate that I had knocked on the doors of around 300
houses before I hit possible pay dirt. A woman who had lived in the
neighborhood all her life - over 60 years - stared at my photograph
and said that, although she didn't know who the kid was, for sure,
it kind of reminded her of the little boy on the next block who was
killed back in the 50's some time. She couldn't remember the details,
but she said it was big news at the time. I asked her if she recalled
how he was killed.

"Yeah. In fact this tricycle reminded me; he was killed when he
had an accident trying to ride his bike down a steep hill they used to
call 'Devil's Slide,' I think it was."

"Devil's Slide?"

"Something like that. It's still there, if you want to go see it."

Indeed I did. "How do I get there?"

"You go north up Conyer, here, for a few blocks then turn right
at Murray and go about a mile and half. You can't miss it."

That turned out to be an understatement. When I reached the
spot called "Devil's Slide," I found it was a very steep hill. In fact, I
don't think I've ever seen such a steep stretch of road in an urban or
suburban setting. It looked a lot like a street in San Francisco, except
even steeper. Today, there were homes and a few small business
located here; but back in the 50's, the lady told me, it was out in the
boondocks. I had a vague recollection that I had known about it when
I was a kid, living a few miles away in Oak Hill. But I never ventured
to take my bike there. If I had, I would have remembered this place.
It was scary enough driving down it in a car; you would never have

gotten me to coast down it on a bicycle. When I got to the opposite side of the hill, I pulled over to think about it. How likely was it that this angelic-looking kid on his tricycle, about 4 or 5 years old, as far as I could tell, would end up flying 60 miles an hour down this hill? And how old was he if and when it happened?

14

The next logical step was to drive over to the north side of the freeway and visit Redwood High School. There were no students around, because it was Christmas vacation, but some of the administrative staff was there and a few conscientious teachers were toiling away on their precious bulletin boards. The first thing I asked the secretary was how old the school was. She said it was built in 1910. So I asked to see somebody who might possibly dig up a copy of the school yearbooks for the years from about 1951 through 1955. It turned out that their library had a whole row of yearbooks, dating clear back to the 20's, so I took the five that seemed most promising and sat down at a big empty table and started to go through them.

First, I managed to find all three of the murder victims: Violet Strand, and Walter Knob in their individual class pictures in '55; and Prospero on the football team in the '54 yearbook.

I next went through the yearbooks looking for any indication of the accomplishments or activities of Strand and Knobb, neither of whom had participated in any extracurricular activities of note; though Prospero had been on the JV football team. Strand showed up in the Home Economics class picture, as well as the Latin class photo. Prospero was in the "Gearheads" - members of the auto shop class; and, of course on the football team. Knobb I couldn't find in any clubs. The overall picture was of high school students on the academic periphery; not brains; not soshes - just kids who went to school and came home without significantly affecting the ebb and flow of social, academic, or athletic life at Redwood High School, with the exception of Prospero. The next thing I did was thumb through all the yearbooks from 1951 to 1955, checking out candid shots around campus and at the proms that usually fill two or three pages of most high school yearbooks. It was difficult, because the only thing I had to go by was how they looked in their class pictures, which are often not how they looked every day, and certainly not how they looked at their demise. I could get a pretty good look at some of the kids at the dances, and a few in the random candid shots, but none stood out as possibilities. I had just about given up when I noticed, at the back of the 1954 yearbook, where they had photos of students standing outside some business establishments that were advertising in the book, a group of four kids lounging in front of a Foster's Freeze place. One of them caught my eye, because his crooked nose and extremely high flattop haircut looked just like the photo of Walter Knobb in his class picture. So I kept turning back and forth between the pictures and, sure enough, that was Knobb. But that's not all. Two of the others looked a lot like the photos of Strand and Prospero. I checked them out carefully, and, although I couldn't be as sure as I was with Knobb, they, too, could definitely have been the same kids; the fourth was definitely not familiar. It occurred to me that it would be very coincidental for three of the four who were clustered together to look so much like the class photos of my murder victims. I couldn't positively identify them, but, as I always say, coincidence is evidence. Intriguingly, the caption at the bottom of the ad read "The Four Musketeers" enjoy Foster's chocolate chip cones." I now strongly suspected that all three of my murder victims had been acquainted, if not intimately connected while in high school. And if that was the case, the motive for their murders had to be many years old, especially since Gordon Prospero left town in 1955 and never returned.

It was the fourth person in the picture - a boy - who most intrigued me. Who was he? How was he connected to the other three, if at all? Was I looking at my killer, perhaps, or a future victim? As tired as I was with having to go over and over all these yearbook pictures, I knew I wouldn't be at ease until I did what I could to find out who he was. He was a big, bulky, kid who looked to me like a wannabe athlete; so I immediately turned to the sports pages. Given his size, I started with the photos of the football teams to see if he was identifiable. In the 1954 yearbook, I found what appeared to be him in the back row of the same junior varsity football team as Prospero. I checked on the list of last names at the bottom and came up with someone surnamed "Matcher". Cross-checking with class pictures, I found Cory Matcher, who clearly had difficulty smiling when having his picture taken, much like myself.

I was fortunate that there would be very few Matchers, especially Cory Matchers, in the whole country, much less the San Joaquin Valley. I went through the Tulare and Visalia phone books and found no Matchers. I tried the Bakersfield and Fresno phone books in the library and had no better luck. Just for the heck of it, after I got home that night, I checked my on my local Oak Hill phone book. Voila! Eureka! I found it. Not only was there a Matcher, his first name was Cory, and he lived only about a quarter mile from me. Detectives not only have to be good, they have to be lucky.

15

It was about 8:00 P.M., past dinnertime, when I got to Cory Matcher's home. A woman who appeared to be in her mid-50's answered the door. She wore a loose-fitting, flowered house dress and her grayish, dirty-blonde hair was pulled back into a ponytail. When I asked if Cory Matcher lived there, she said that he was her husband, and she called to him. The man who ambled from the kitchen was tall, maybe 6'3", and corpulent, with rolls of fat draped over his belt. He was completely bald, and had a short, salt-and-pepper beard. He squinted like he needed glasses. He hadn't bothered to pull his lounging robe closed. He was wearing boxer shorts and flip-flops. He didn't invite me in, at first. When I told him who I was he reluctantly waved me in, but did not invite me to sit. I remained standing, as did his wife, evidently expecting bad news, as though this wasn't the first time they'd been visited by a policeman. He, too, seemed a bit tense, as though waiting for a hammer to drop.

"Mister Matcher, let me get right to the point. Did you know Violet Strand, Gordon Prospero, or Walter Knobb?"

He stared at me for several seconds, seeming to be trying to decide something. Then he drawled, "Yeah, I knew'em a long time ago, when we were kids."

"Did you know they were recently murdered?"

He dropped heavily into a plush, well-worn couch, then wrestled his body up into more upright sitting position.

"I knew about Vi and Walt 'cuz I read it in the paper, but yer sayin' Gordy was killed, too?"

"Yes, in Oak Hill." I lied about that to gauge his response. He showed no reaction. He either didn't know Prospero had been killed in Phoenix, or he was a much cooler customer than I gave him credit for on first glance. In any event: "Vi," "Walt," and "Gordy"? These four had known each other very well. He started to stand again, but suddenly, his legs got weak and he plopped back down, again. So, I looked around, found a dining room chair, and sat, uninvited.

He started telling me the story of the "Four Musketeers."

"Me and Gordy and Vi and Walt used to hang out together from the time Gordy was in the sixth grade and we were in the fifth. We stayed friends all the way through high school. But after Gordy left town, we all sort of drifted apart. We weren't whatcha would call typical high school students. None of us fit in with the 'in crowd.' I played a little football and Vi was the only one of us who was a half way decent student. We didn't really fit in at Redwood, though, so we just sort of kept to ourselves. We got into a little bit of trouble now and then, like getting caught smoking under the bleachers, or ditching school, dumb stuff like that. But we never did anything bad. We just didn't have much to do with any of the other kids; that's why we took to calling ourselves 'The Four Musketeers,' I guess."

"Actually, there were only three musketeers, plus D'Artagnan. Which one of you was him? He? Which one was D'Artagnan?"

"Ha, ha, that would be me, I guess." That seemed to relax him a little.

I pulled out my little photo.

"Do you by any chance recognize this kid?"

He looked at it with evident seriousness and no apparent recognition and said, "I don't think so."

"What if I told you he was killed when riding a bike down 'Devil's Slide' over in East Visalia?"

That's when D'Artagnan dropped his sword. He was unable to hide his sudden shock, but then he made a bigger mistake; he said that he didn't remember anything like that. If he had said that he remembered it vaguely, or something similar, he could easily have gotten away with the lie. But his shocked reaction told me that he not only remembered it but he didn't want me to know it.

Still, he recovered well and continued the bluff, which I decided not to interrupt. I figured the longer he talked, the more he would unintentionally reveal. So I primed the pump.

"I've been told this kid here actually tried to ride his bike down 'Devil's Slide'."

"Hey, this kid here couldn't be more than six. I never even learned to ride a bike till I was eight. It wasn't on this tricycle was it? What does this have to do with the murders?"

"You think this kid looks like he's six? He doesn't look to me to be much more than four."

"I can't tell; it's a pretty old picture."

"How do you know that? It looks kind of new to me." I was showing him the one I figured was a recent copy.

"I dunno, it just looks old, to me."

"It was probably taken two or three years before he was killed."

That's when he stopped talking and waited for me to say something, because, I thought, he really wanted to know for sure the answer to the question of just who this kid was. And why would that answer be so important to him? Could he be the murderer and was trying to pry information out of me about where I was in my investigation? Or maybe he was involved somehow in the kid's death and was beginning to worry that somebody was out to get him in trouble. I didn't give him any answers, though, because I didn't have any. And he didn't appear likely to be more forthcoming until I could hit him again with more details.

"Well, Mister Matcher, thanks for your help. I'll be getting back to you." If he was involved in some way, he was going to lose some sleep over wondering just how much I knew, which was nothing more than I'd already told him, really.

When I went to bed that night, I couldn't sleep, either. The interview with Cory Matcher was certainly enlightening, insofar as it gave me the sense that I was on the right track. All good detectives can spot a liar, and Cory, I was certain was lying, or at least was avoiding the truth. But so what? His lies weren't evidence of a crime that he might have committed, witnessed, or heard about. But the thing that bothered me most was the chance that, if Cory Matcher was a killer, he might kill again before I stopped him. Or if he was a potential victim of a killer, how could I protect him? If I warned him of possible danger, and it turned out that he was the killer, I would have given away my advantage. On the other hand, what if he were to be murdered because I had kept silent... By morning, I had made up my mind. Just as it's better to let a guilty man go free than to convict an innocent one, it was equally better to save the life of a potential victim even if I had to risk alerting a killer that I was on to him. As soon as I was finished with breakfast, I went back to the Matchers' house. He and his wife were not happy to see me, but they allowed me in.

"Mister Matcher," I began, "I regret to have to tell you this, but I fear your life might be in danger."

This did not seem to shock him; either he knew he wasn't in danger because he was the killer, or he had probably been thinking the same thing, all night and was numb to it, In any case, he said nothing.

"As you know, three of your childhood friends have been murdered, and there's reason to believe it has something to do with the death of this kid on his tricycle in the picture, years ago. My best advice to you is make certain that, every night, you lock all your doors and windows securely."

"What about Marie?"

"Marie? Oh you mean your wife?"

"That's right. Should I send her some place else where it's safer?"

"That's up to you; I doubt that this killer is interested in killing her, though. Besides, so far, all the murders were committed when the victim was alone. Having someone else with you might discourage a potential killer. Of course, if you know some place where your wife can be safer, maybe you should go there, too."

"I hadn't thought of that. I'll think about it."

"Good. I feel better knowing you're going to be careful."

"Chief Crockett, do you have any idea who might be doing these killings?"

"Well, ma'am, I hate to tell you this, but the best suspect I have, so far, is your husband."

"ME! Why me?"

"Look, Mister Matcher, There were four of you in your group of 'musketeers', and three of you are dead. That makes you what we call, a 'person of interest'. If I were you, I'd start trying to establish exactly where you were when the killings were done."

"Do you know the dates?"

"Not off the top of my head, I'm embarrassed to say. All I can tell you is that they were committed over a period of about a month, starting in early October. If you call me at the Oak Hill Police Department I can give you the exact times and dates."

"What do you think I should do?"

"For starters, you should tell me the truth about what you know about this kid's death."

He put his head down and started to breathe hard.

"Tell him, Cory! You want to get killed because of some psycho out to get you?"

"I can't, Marie, not yet."

"Can't you at least tell me the kid's name?"

"No, I really don't remember."

"He's telling the truth, sir. Whenever we've talked about this before, he just called him 'that little kid'."

"Look, Chief Crockett, all I can tell you right now is that the kid who was killed was older than this one in the picture. And I really don't know his name, and it happened a long time ago. If you can come back later after I've had a chance to think about it and remember everything that happened better, I'll be glad to tell you."

They clearly were anxious for me to leave. I couldn't think of anything else useful to ask them, just now, so I left with a final warning:

"Okay, Mister Matcher, I can't arrest you for anything, but I'm counting on you to be cooperative; in the meantime, watch your back."

So, the pieces were falling into place on my puzzle; but the next key piece, I was sure, would be the name of the kid. So how would I get that? My first thought was the newspaper archives; but first, Harry and Bud had been working on finding more information about Walter Knobb and were showing their copy of the photo around, I hoped maybe they had already found out who the kid was and would save me a lot of shoe leather. Unfortunately, the only person I had found when I canvassed the area around the "Flying 'A'" station who had lived there half a century ago had no idea of the name of the kid on the tricycle.

16

When I got to Tom's office, Harry and Bud had already finished finding and interviewing a number of people associated with victim #2, Walter Knobb, and came up with next to nothing useful, except that a couple of them looked high on something.

"Okay, Arnie, here's what we got, so far: He wasn't exactly Mister Clean, but he operated close enough to the legal fence, so to speak, that he managed to stay out of jail. His neighbors say he smoked a lot of pot, and that some drug dealer used to come by regularly. Thought he was Chinese, or Japanese, or something."

"Really? You know an Asian man was seen loitering around Strand's house."

"That's right, you mentioned that before. I guess we need to check that out. But that's not all; our Mister Knobb was a horse player, and was constantly in debt to bookies."

"Interesting, but bookies hardly ever kill their customers and their customers' friends. I'm pretty sure that's a blind alley"

"One more thing," added Bud, "hardly anybody liked him; not the neighbors, and not his relatives. None of them were exactly doubled over with grief at his demise."

"Well, no matter how many motives we come up with, we would still have to connect them to the other victims who, as far as we know, were not involved with drugs, gambling, or any other illegal activities. And what local bookie or drug dealer would go all the way to Phoenix to kill Gordon Prospero? That makes absolutely no sense."

"You're probably right. You come up with anything, so far?"

"Yeah, I did, Harry. Our three victims were close friends in high school with another guy named Cory Matcher who is still very much alive and living just a few blocks from me, as it happens. Not only that, but he knows something about the kid in the photo, even though I'm sure he's holding something back. He claims not to know the kid's name, but I'm not so sure. Did you guys show your copy around?"

"Yeah. Nobody has a clue."

17

So, it was back to the drawing board, as far as finding out who the kid in the photo was. For all I knew, he was someone who was still alive. Maybe he was the killer, leaving a picture of himself at each scene just to show off how much smarter he is than the cops and taunting them. In my gut, though, I thought he was the kid who was killed on "Devil's Slide," so many years ago. The fact that Cory thought this kid looked like he was about 6, made me suspect that he was subconsciously giving me something closer to the actual age of the kid when he was killed on a bicycle.

Before I forgot it, I called Cory Matcher on the phone and gave him the dates of all the murders so he could try to account for his whereabouts at the time the killings took place. Being aware that I was giving him an opportunity to fabricate alibis, I deliberately did not tell him yet that one of the victims, Gordon Prospero had been killed in Phoenix. That meant that, for that murder, his alibi could be more easily disproved if it were false, because he would have to account for his movements over about a two day period, which he was probably not prepared to lie about. As it happened, Cory claimed he was working every day and had no time to be killing people. That didn't prevent him from doing the deed late at night, of course; but, if true, working would be a good alibi for the Prospero murder, since it would not allow him time to travel to Phoenix, commit Prospero's murder, and return to work. That suggested to me that he was either innocent, or a lot smarter than he appeared.

I headed next to the offices of the Visalia Times-Delta, the principal daily newspaper for Tulare County. I spent a couple of hours scrolling through their microfiche records of old newspapers. Unfortunately, the records prior to 1960 were spotty, with some missing, and none of the ones they had on file included any mention of a kid being killed going down a mountain road. I spent two days going through these records, as well as those of the Porterville Recorder, and the Bakersfield Californian. I even tried The Sun-Gazette in Lindsay. It's just a small weekly, but it's about as close to "Devil's Slide" as is Visalia. Actually, Exeter is closer still, but I couldn't find any newspaper office there. I thought sure at least one of these papers would have an old copy with the story of the accident, but I thought wrong.

I had wasted two days. Now I really had to think out of the box. Then I got an idea. At first, it seemed like a desperation move; but the more I thought about it, the more it seemed like it would work. I went back to the high school and pulled out a single yearbook -1952, when I knew all my victims, as well as Cory Matcher, were students there. Matcher had already made a de facto admission that the death of the kid was something he knew about, and it would most likely have been when he was in high school. What I did was go though the entire student body looking up each name of a male student that I could cross-reference with the Visalia phone book. It took three hours of looking back and forth between the yearbook and the phonebook, but I finally came up with a list of 19 male students. The reason I only looked up male students was that female students would mostly have different last names today from the ones they had then. I then simply called each of the men up on the phone and asked him one simple question: "Do you remember back when you were a kid, when a little boy was killed riding a bike down 'Devil's slide'? Out of the 19 I called, 14 were at home. Out of those 14, 8 remembered the incident. But out of those 8, none could remember the kid's name. When I hung up on that last call, I was very disappointed. As I drove back to my office in Oak Hill, I tried to think of some other way, but came up dry.

As soon as I walked into my police station, Irma informed me that someone had called with important information about some kid's death and left a number to call back, which I did, immediately.

"Hello, Mister Olney?"

"Yes?"

This is Constable Crockett; did you leave a message for me to call?"

"Oh, yes, chief. After you called, I realized that there was somebody who knew that kid's name - my mother."

"Your mother's still alive?"

"Yes, she is, and still quite sharp mentally, at 83."

"And did she remember who the kid was?"

"She said his name was Ronald Schlesinger, S-C-H-L-E-S-I-N-G-E R."

"Did she remember anything else?"

"Only that witnesses said that he tried to coast his bike down 'Devil's Slide' and lost control going maybe fifty miles an hour. Broke most every bone in his body."

"So your mother wasn't a witness?"

"No, but she understood there were some local kids watched it happen."

"Did she remember how old he was?"

"She was pretty sure he was six or seven."

"Really?"

"Sounds kind of young to be doing that, doesn't it?"

I was thinking that I, like Cory Matcher, never even learned to ride a bike till I was 8.

"Does your mother know who any of these witnesses who saw it happen were?"

"No, can't help you there. My mom wasn't there when it happened. She only read about it in the Times-Delta. It just said witnesses, but she didn't think it named any of them. You know, because they were kids."

"One more thing: does she remember the year?"

"She said it was 1949."

18

Back at my office, I sat at my desk staring at the photo of the kid on the tricycle, trying to put together in my head a bunch of jigsaw puzzle pieces that were not yet forming a discernible picture. Most of the pieces might join together in one of the pictures I had in mind; but they might also join in an entirely different picture that hadn't yet occurred to me. What it all came down to was that I had only two definite clues in this case: the photo and the "four musketeers." That the photo was unquestionably linked to the murders in some way, and that the "musketeers" were also linked with the death of this kid; it was the only explanation I could come up with for why it had been left at every murder scene except Tom's. And the fact that three of the "4 musketeers" had been murdered in the same manner, and that one of them had left town almost 40 years before and had never returned, was pretty solid evidence that the motive for the murders originated 40 or more years ago - a motive that didn't include Tom.

What it all boiled down to, I thought, was that my next step would have to be to confirm, once and for all, whether or not the kid on the tricycle was Ronald Schlesinger. If so, it meant that Ronald was very likely a part of the motive for the killings. If I could establish that as an unambiguous fact, I would have taken a big leap forward. Unfortunately, the only evidence I had that these two kids were one and the same was the one person I located in Visalia who thought it "looked a lot like" the kid who had been killed all those years ago. And if the lady who says this happened in 1949 is correct, that meant my witness who tentatively ID'd the photo was operating from a 44 year old memory - hardly air-tight. It also suggested that the "four musketeers" were most likely in junior high school when Ronald died. I decided that I had to find a way to determine for certain whether or not this kid I was staring at was Ronald Schlesinger. Without that fact being established, there was no way to link the killer to the death of the kid on "Devil's Slide." Then into my office walked a monkey wrench; TWO monkey wrenches, to be exact, and their names were Laurel & Hardy.

19

Two and half years earlier, I had run into these two ATF agents while investigating the murder of my childhood friend, Eddie South, who had this job before I did. They had harassed me because they felt that I, a civilian, had no business interfering with their investigation of the same murder. The agents had it linked in their minds with drug trafficking in Tulare County. It turned out they were wrong, though, and they left town before I ever learned their names.

The following year, while I was trying to find out who killed two local teachers, they showed up again. This time, though, they were on the right track, because I had determined that the killer was part of an anti-government, religious cult that was under investigation for federal crimes. And this time, they couldn't have been more helpful, and we became friends.

"Well," said Arthur Grainger (Laurel), "we're going to have to stop meeting like this." Arthur was kind of gangly, if a middle-aged person could be called "gangly." He was rail thin, with wispy, steel gray hair that constantly fell in strands over his face, which was perpetually shaded in a five o-clock shadow. Although the two agents were of equal rank, and "Hardy" was the more assertive of the two, it was Arthur who seemed to more carefully weigh options and to make most of their decisions.

"How ya doin', chief," said Myron Mesmer (Hardy). Like his namesake, Myron was on the beefy side - probably on the borderline of what the ATF would accept in their ranks. He seemed to favor the color black. His hair was black. His eyes were so dark brown that they blended with the pupils to give the impression that all he had was a cornea and a very large pupil. It looked like he could hypnotize someone with those eyes, which was kind of a disquieting thought, since he claimed to be related to the inventor of hypnotism, Franz Anton Mesmer. He was barrel-chested and possessed thick, muscular, upper arms. Whenever he reached forward it always appeared that his coat - black - was about to split the seams in the back. His shoes - black patent leather looked expensive.

"Well, if I'm not mistaken, this is a pair of Janet Reno's boys come to pay me a visit."

"Sure, why else would we come to this one-horse town, pardner?"

"My guess, Myron? drugs, again."

"Partly, but also because of Tom's murder."

"Seems like everybody in the world knows about it."

"You'll have to get out more, Arnie. Tom's murder was mentioned on the "Today" show, because he made such a big impression on Jane and Bryant when he was their guest."

"Jane and Bryant? So you're bosom buddies now, are you?"

"Sure, they don't do nothing without checking with us, first."

"Ha ha, very funny. But you said you're here on a drug investigation, too?"

"Same investigation, actually. ATF headquarters got a tip that Tom was killed by drug kingpins, along with some local small-timer who was killed for not paying up."

"Let me guess again: Walter Knobb."

"That's the dude," said Myron, without elaboration. "Anyhow, we had our main suspect under surveillance because we didn't have enough evidence for a warrant, when who do we see walking up to his front door? Chief Constable Arnie Crockett of Oak Hill."

"You were surveilling Cory Matcher?"

"That's the guy," said Myron, still without providing any detail

"Well, far be it from me to tell you you're barking up the wrong tree, but I've interviewed him twice, now, and he's the furthest thing I could imagine from a drug lord. A killer, possibly, but I can't picture this couch potato having the energy to run a drug cartel of some kind."

"So why are you interested in him?"

"Because three people have been murdered so far, besides Tom, and he's a good candidate for being either their killer or a potential fourth victim. The four of them were tight years ago."

"You said there were others besides Tom and Knobb who were killed?"

"You didn't know that? Who gave you this tip?"

"We don't know. Our boss just said it was an anonymous tip from someone who sounded credible."

"Man or woman?"

"Don't know, yet."

"Just so you'll know. A woman named Violet Strand was killed nearby in Visalia; and a man named Gordon Prospero was killed in Phoenix. Strand, Knobb, and Tom were all killed with the same gun, a .22. Ballistics in Phoenix says his killing was with a different gun - a .32."

"Phoenix? How would that be connected to these other murders?"

"Knobb, Strand, and Prospero were friends in high school, along with guess who?"

"Cory Matcher, right?"

"On the nose, Myron."

"And Tom?" interjected Arthur.

"Wrong place at the wrong time. I think he was getting too close."

"Rotten shame," said Myron.

"Well, I'll have to thank you guys. Just as I was getting discouraged from the lack of clues in this case, you two come along and give me another piece for my puzzle - an important one, I suspect."

"We gave you a clue?"

"I think so. I think your tipster is up to his earlobes in these murders. I think he was just trying to throw off investigators. If he decided that Matcher would be too difficult to get to, since he is always either at work or with his wife, he may have decided that maybe he could frame him somehow. That way, he would not only keep suspicion off himself, but still get revenge on Matcher. It's a theory. I don't know about drugs, though. In the two years I've been chief I haven't heard the slightest rumble about drug dealing anywhere closer than Porterville."

"Now that you mention it, we've got a couple of agents on permanent stakeout at the Porterville airport, watching for suspicious planes."

"Anything yet?"

"Not yet. But that's how we believe most Illegal shipments come into the San Joaquin Valley."

We kicked around old times a bit, if you can call the last couple of years "old times," and the two agents got up to leave.

"Well, Arnie," said Myron, "you seem to have clues you want to follow, and we need to get back to our drug investigation, so we'll leave you to your jigsaw puzzle."

"Yeah, see you guys, later. Keep me up to date on what you're finding, and I'll do the same."

After they left, I gave no thought whatsoever to drugs, and sat down and stared at my photo again. I knew for a certainty that I couldn't make any more progress without positively identifying this kid. But how?

20

The next thing I decided to try was a return visit to the offices of the Visalia Times Delta. This newspaper had been in operation only a short distance from where the "Devil's Slide" tragedy had taken place; they MUST have covered it at the time. I was overly optimistic. This time, though the people working at the paper searched diligently through their files and archived copies of old papers, they still found nothing.

I was sure some older folks in Visalia must know who this kid in the photo was. Or perhaps is. I felt it was most likely Ronald Schlesinger, but "most likely" doesn't solve cases. There HAD to be a way to find people who knew for sure. I obviously couldn't go door-to-door through all of Visalia.

Then it hit me. I didn't know why I hadn't thought of it before. Instead of going around knocking on doors, I could locate the school this kid likely attended and go from there. First of all, this little boy, who evidently rode or walked his bike to the steep hill where he died almost certainly lived in that area. If he was only seven, he is not likely to have come a long way. So I called the Visalia Unified School District offices and they informed me that the school nearest "Devil's Slide," which apparently everyone in town knew about, was the Goshen Elementary School, which was about a mile away from where the kid was killed. There was a very good chance he had been a student there.

When I parked in front of the school, it looked to me to be old enough to have been there in 1949. It was all gray walls - a cement/plaster compound of some sort. The windows were all small-paned in wooden frames. The main entrance was fronted by a solid cement arch. I introduced myself to the principal, Audrey Turner. She had light brown, shoulder-length hair, pulled back tightly. She appeared to be in her late 30's, dressed pretty much as one would expect of a school principal, complete with half-glasses, over which she looked at me appraisingly.

"Thank you very much Missus Turner for speaking with me."

"Happy to be of assistance if I can, Chief Crockett; and it's 'Miss'".

"Oh, sorry about that."

"Don't worry about it. You're kind of famous around here, especially when they talked about you on the 'Today' show. And here you are - the chief over in Oak Hill. How can I help?"

I was getting kind of tired being reminded that I wasn't actually on the "Today" show myself because I was afraid to fly. Given the attention I was already receiving for my non-appearance, imagine what a celebrity I would be if I had flown to New York. But if I had, the plane probably would have crashed.

"Well, first of all, how did this school get named 'Goshen'?"

"I don't know, exactly, but I think it has something to do with someplace in Egypt that's mentioned in the Bible."

"Huh. Well, first of all, are you aware of the fact that a boy was killed trying to ride his bike down "Devil's Slide," back in 1949?"

"Yes, I am. In fact, over the years, many of our students have been seriously injured trying to ride their bikes down that hill. I believe he was the only one ever killed, though."

"He was a student here, then?"

"I'm sorry, I don't know."

"I don't suppose you know what his name was?"

"No, I wasn't even alive at the time. I'm sure there are others who know, though." She got up, walked to her door and addressed the secretary in the outer office. "Olive!"

The elderly secretary looked up. "Olive, dear, you've been here a lot longer than I. Do you remember the little boy who was killed going down Devil's Slide.'?"

"I vaguely recall mention of it."

"Was he one of ours?"

"Sorry, ma'am, couldn't tell you."

"Any idea who might know?"

"Can't help you there, either."

"Was this school around in '49?"

"It was built in 1936, actually."

"Well, Miss Turner, if he was as young as it appears, and he took his bike to 'Devil's Slide', it is logical to assume that this kid must have lived nearby. So, it seems likely he might have been a student, here, right?"

"He could have been, I suppose, but I don't know if he was."

"Do you keep class pictures from past years?"

"Yes, we do. What was the boy's name."

"Ronald Schlesinger, I think."

I pulled out my photo and set it on her desk. "Oh, I see, this is the child?"

"I don't know that, for sure, either. But I thought that if you had old class photos, I could go through them and try to match this picture with class pictures. They are usually taken by professional photographers and are pretty sharp. The one I have here isn't quite so sharp, but sharp enough for a comparison, I think."

"Well, in this picture, he looks like he might have been in kindergarten or first grade when it was taken. That would make it around 1946 or '47."

"That's what I was thinking. Do you think you might have class pictures from that far back?"

"As a matter of fact, we have them all the way back to when the school opened, though I can't be sure that there aren't any missing. Not only that, but many, in fact most, of the photos don't have the names of the students on them."

Sorry to hear that. Could we look at them anyway?"

"Sure, wait right here a few minutes. They're filed away in the storeroom."

I found my knees bouncing like pistons a little in anticipation of her return. When she did come back, she was carrying a cardboard

box full of class pictures, filed by year. This box was from the '40's.
I started with kindergarten classes - two of them - from 1946. Miss
Turner and I looked at each photo carefully, trying to find any kid
who looked remotely like the one in my photo. In one picture, a
couple of kids looked a little like mine, but enough different to not be
definitive. After carefully studying the two kindergarten classes, we
pulled out the first grade classes - two of them as well. But in neither
of the 1946 photos did we find any clear matches. Then we got out
the ones from 1947. After striking out on the kindergarten photos, I
struck pay dirt on the one of a first grade class. In the first photo I
looked at, at the right end of the first row, a boy was kneeling who
looked very much like my picture. Miss Turner got out a magnifying
glass and we took turns studying both photos very carefully. The
deciding factor was that, in both pictures, the boy had a blemish of
some kind - a mole, or a birthmark on his neck that I hadn't noticed
until I saw it with a good magnifying glass. And the marks were in
EXACTLY the same location on his neck. It looked a little like the
liver spot on my forehead. I had no doubt these boys were the same.
Elation soon gave way to disappointment, though: unfortunately,
there were no names on the pictures or on the back.

"I'm sorry, chief."

"Don't be, yet. Would you happen to have class lists from 1948?"

"Sorry, we don't keep old class lists for more than a couple of
years."

"Okay, NOW you can be sorry."

But it wasn't a total failure, because at least I now knew that the
kid had lived in the immediate neighborhood. Unfortunately, that
also meant I wasn't going to be able to get out of going door to door.

On the one hand, I was spending a lot of time and shoe leather
(shoe rubber, actually) on a single clue. On the other hand, it was the
only clue I had, except for the "four musketeers." And if I came up
empty on linking my photo with the kid who was killed, evidently with
these four witnessing it, I would just have to thoroughly investigate
each of their backgrounds. Perhaps, if I was lucky, Laurel & Hardy
would come up with something I could use vis a vis Cory Matcher,

but I wasn't holding my breath. Harry and Bud were working hard on Walter Knobb's past, but I wasn't too hopeful on that score, either.

I checked in again with the school district to determine the boundaries of the small community served by Goshen Elementary School. Then I started walking from house to house asking the same question: "Did anyone in this house attend Goshen Elementary School in the late 40's?" It took an entire day, but I came up with seven people in the approximate age range to have been in elementary school at that time. I asked each of them two questions: "Do you remember when one of your classmates was killed on 'Devil's Slide'?" They all remembered that traumatic event. Then the big question, as I showed them my photo: "Do you remember his name?"

Bingo!

One woman said, "Of course, that's Ronnie Schlesinger." I felt like jumping up and down in triumph, like Rocky in the movie

"Why are you so sure?"

"We were both in first and second grade together. We liked to play hopscotch at school. Not only that, but he lived down the street from me and we played a lotta games,'specially 'kick-the-can.'"

"That was one of my favorites, too. So where did you live, then?"

"Right here."

"Really?" One of the things about small towns that is different from big cities is that, in places like this, a lot of things remain unchanged for years. This lady had never married, and she just decided to stay put.

"Which house did he live in?"

"It was the third one that way down on the other side of the street, but a lot of different families have lived there since. I don't think any of them could help you."

I didn't think so, either, but I did due diligence and mostly got blank stares. One lady invited me in to look around for clues, but I declined the offer.

21

Finally, my jigsaw puzzle had a coherent picture forming into which I could start fitting my pieces as they became available. The killer had left the same photo at three of his four murders; and that photo, I now knew, was of a kid who had been killed with three of my four murder victims and one of their friends watching. The most likely suspect, now, seemed to be Cory Matcher. And yet, having talked to him twice, my gut feeling was that he wasn't a killer; but he very possibly could be someone the killer wanted to execute in order to put his tortured soul to rest. His problem was that Matcher was not only nearly impossible to find alone in the dead of night like the others, he was somebody I was watching; and he was someone under constant surveillance by the ATF. I figured that gave me some breathing room as I investigated more deeply.

So, for the time being, I decided to set Mr. Matcher aside and concentrate on trying to come up with someone else who might have had a motive for killing the people who were present at Ronald Schlesinger's ugly demise. Certainly anyone who had been there would remember it vividly. And, of course, the first thing you think of is family. Someone had seethed in anger for forty years over this death. Who else but a family member who had been psychologically devastated could have kept that hate inside for so long without doing something about it? Brothers, sisters, parents, relatives or close friends; all were a possibility. But how to narrow down that suspect list? One advantage I had was that the idea of any of the usual motives: sex, money, jealousy, drugs were hard to justify. Harry, Bud, and Laurel & Hardy could look all they wanted in those directions with the backgrounds of the victims, but NONE of those motives fit the facts I had, so far. I had no doubt that the motive was long-festering hatred that, for some reason, had finally erupted in sudden fury all these years later. And the logical place to start looking was at family members. The only thing I had to go on was that their names were probably Schlesinger. Hoping to extend my newfound winning streak, I did check local phone directories. But my lucky streak ended there - no Schlesinger's in this part of the San Joaquin Valley.

By the time I got home that night, I was exhausted and grateful to be settling in for one of Marjorie's great dinners. She covered the dining table with mashed potatoes, gravy, corn on the cob, refried beans, franks, and corned beef hash. I was in hog heaven. Marjorie's son - my deputy, Duane, came to join us for dinner, mostly from force of habit, though he had technically moved out of his mom's house when we got married. As it turned out, I was glad he showed up, because he came up with a theory to challenge mine, and it was worth considering.

"Hey, Arnie, you know there's another possibility you might not have thought about. What if, back in 1949, somebody actually caused this kid's death and there were witnesses who knew about it. Then, recently, one of them confronted the killer and tried to blackmail him? And that ended up dragging in the others? He might be someone whose respect in the community would be threatened by this disclosure, so he might have felt he had to get rid of witnesses he had known about, years ago"

"So what you're saying is that Strand, Knobb, and Prospero had all been witnesses to a killing years ago; and now that one of them, perhaps anonymously, is threatening to blow the whistle, he's decided to kill all of them?"

"That's exactly what I'm saying."

"Well, it's just as good a theory as mine, I guess. You know, Duane, I've been leaving you out of all this. We should be working together. You, me, and your computer might just be able to crack this case.

22

Duane Altmeier was 26. Thin as a rail and wiry, he was nonetheless strong and agile. He could even skateboard proficiently. I can't even stand on one without falling off. His sandy hair constantly fell over his eyes, and his long Henry Fonda stride made him one of the most recognizable presences on the streets of Oak Hill - very well liked by everyone. His father's whereabouts were unknown, having been released from prison about five years earlier after serving time for sexual assaults. He had also physically abused Duane and his mother. Duane hated him. Although I had known Marjorie since the 8th grade, I had never met or known about either Duane or his father. I remember well who her boyfriends had been in junior high school and high school, but she evidently ran into this bonehead after graduation and after I had left town. But Marjorie's loving and steady hand had managed to raise a truly smart, admirable, stalwart son despite her asshole husband. Duane had been my late friend Eddie's most trusted deputy, and now he was mine. I had no doubt that he would soon become the next Chief Constable as I spent most of my time hiking around Wolfskill Peak. If I'd had my druthers, I would have chosen to eventually die on one of these hikes and let the coyotes have at me. Of course, that had almost happened on the day I caught Eddie's killer just below the peak. Back at the office the next day, Duane and I huddled in my office and brainstormed.

"Okay, Duane, I like your theory of how Cory Matcher might have had a good motive for these murders. In fact, so far, he's the only person I can think of who even might have a motive. So the first thing I think we should do is give him a surprise return visit and ask him for his alibis. I told him the dates of the killings, so he should have come up with alibis by now, assuming he has any. The killings all took place late at night, so if he has a day job, I don't see how he could have killed Gordon Prospero if he was at work that day But we don't know for certain that there is only one killer. The murder in Phoenix was done with a different weapon than the ones here."

"You warned him beforehand?"

"I know, that sounds like I'm giving him advanced warning and all. But, first of all, I did not tell him that one of the killings was in Phoenix, so he won't be expecting that he would have to come up with an alibi covering two days if he's innocent. And if he DOES hit us with a two-day alibi to cover the Prospero murder, that's suggestive of guilt, since I didn't tell him he would need one."

"Good thinking, chief."

"Thanks. Now, let's assume for the moment that Matcher isn't guilty. Then we need to come up with a way to determine who else might have had a reason to kill these three friends from over forty years ago."

"And, knowing you, you don't think it could be some kind of coincidence."

"Exactly. Any ideas?"

"Tell me again about how this kid in the photo fits in."

So I went through the whole story in all the detail I could think of.

"Well," Duane said, "I agree with you, it seems to me that we need to start with the family. If somebody forty plus years down the road is still so angry about this kid's death and he believes it was intentional, a family member who really loved him would be by far the one with the strongest motive."

"You don't think it could be a friend, or maybe a former policeman, linked with Tom or something?"

"Pretty much of a stretch, if you ask me."

"I think so, too; so let's concentrate on that angle. Our first job will be to find out the kid's family history. The only thing we know so far is his likely family name - Schlesinger."

"Jewish, maybe?"

"Maybe. And in a redneck, agricultural town like this, that fact - if it is a fact - could be significant. There are a lot of bigots in this area, though they mostly hate Mexicans and Japanese."

"But bigots tend to hate everybody they think is different from them."

"True enough. Well, any notions on how we dig up this kid's family history."

"I've got my computer and Lexis-Nexis."

"Just what I was thinking, and while you concentrate on that, I just thought of another angle: a doctor who might have been this family's physician years ago."

"Still around after forty years?"

"Sounds unlikely, doesn't it? But Doctor Weems, who brought me into the world almost 60 years ago is still alive and occasionally sees patients."

"Yeah, that still blows my mind."

"Anyhow, I think it's worth a try."

"I have another suggestion: how about checking synagogues?"

"I didn't think of that. Is there a synagogue in Visalia?"

"Actually, there are two that I know of; one on Chinowith Street called 'B'nai David,' and one called 'Beth Shalom' on Paseo Avenue."

"You never fail to amaze me, Duane. But first things first. Let's both of us go talk to Mister Matcher."

23

Cory Matcher didn't seem too surprised to see us. "Come in, Chief Crockett."

"Thank you. This is Deputy Altmeier."

"I guess you want to know where I was on those dates you gave me."

His wife, Marie walked in, drying her hands on a dishtowel.

"Yes, but the main one I want to know about is October 22; that was a Friday."

"I was at work. In fact, I was at work on all the dates you gave me."

Actually, this would not have been an alibi for three of the murders, because they occurred late at night. However, if he was at work at all on October 22, he could hardly have gotten to Phoenix, committed the murder, and gotten back for work the next morning.

"I'm sorry, Mister Matcher, but it was careless of me to have not asked your occupation before now." I must admit that I just sort of assumed he was the couch potato he appeared to be, 24/7.

"I'm a mechanic at Jiffy-Lube."

"And where is that located?"

"Just down the road, that direction a mile or so." He pointed south.

"Right. I know where that is. Well, that's all we need for now, Mister Matcher; thanks for your cooperation."

"Sure, anytime. You know, I'd like to know myself who killed my friends. They were the best friends I ever had."

Then I hit him with a surprise that caught him completely off guard.

"Cory, do you remember Ronald Schlesinger?"

For a moment, I thought he was going to collapse. He was wobbly and choked on the words he was trying to get out. He was obviously calculating the wisdom of lying, but realized that it would only get him deeper in trouble.

"Ronald Schlesinger? Oh, you mean Ronnie?"

"That's right. Was he a friend of yours, too?"

"Yeah, I guess."

"But the last time I talked to you, you said "But as near as I have been able to find out, he was four or five years younger than you; how did you happen to be friends?"

"I guess 'friends' was the wrong word. I remember him from around the neighborhood."

"But when I showed you his picture the other day, you didn't say anything about it being Ronald Schlesinger. You just called him a 'little kid." I glanced at Marie, and she seemed just as surprised as i was."

"Hey, that picture was of a much younger kid; I just didn't recognize him."

"But you knew about the kid who was killed on 'Devil's Slide'; Are you telling me you didn't know that was Ronald Schlesinger, even though you say you knew him pretty well?"

"Well, you got me all confused; I didn't know what I was saying."

"So it appears. Look, Cory, we're going over to Jiffy-Lube right now to check your alibis, but we'll be back. I'd strongly advise you to think very carefully and remember everything you can about what happened to this kid and how you and your friends fit into the picture. Remember, whoever is killing your old friends may very well be after you, as well."

"Look, I'll help any way I can, honest."

"We're counting on it."

Duane and I headed straight for the Jiffy-Lube about a mile away,.

"That was a pretty short interrogation."

"Well, look at it this way; if his alibi checks out that will save us a lot of questions the next time we talk to him."

"So you're not done with him?"

"Absolutely not. I have little doubt that he holds the key to this whole thing, whether he knows it or not."

24

When we got back to the office after getting a solid confirmation that Cory was working on all the dates of the murders, Duane went to his cubicle, fired up his MacIntosh Computer, and accessed Lexis-Nexis. He started by entering the name "Ronald Schlesinger" into the records of birth and death certificates and general vital statistics. I figured he would be busy with that for a while, so I set out into the big, bad, world of police flatfoot investigations.

I started with a return visit to Goshen Elementary School, which looked so much like the elementary school I had attended in Oak Hill that I wondered if it weren't built by the same architects, and it gave me a vaguely uncomfortable feeling, since I had hated school. To me, school was little more than an interlude between my idyllic early childhood and when I finally started becoming educated after that twelve year waste of time.

But I digress. I wanted to see if the principal had found any class lists including Schlesinger's who had been students there in the 40's through the '60's, hoping to identify a brother or sister. But she had found none.

Next, I headed over to Redwood High School. There were five high schools in Visalia, but, if the Schlesinger's lived in the Goshen Elementary School area, any children from that neighborhood would have most likely attended Redwood. The school librarian was very helpful. An aged, arthritic Miss Crowley pulled every kind of record she could think of and came up with two Schlesinger's who had been students in 1950, '57, and '62, but we couldn't think of any way to connect any of them with Ronald, who, of course, had become deceased when he was still in elementary school. I made a note to give these names to Duane. The students were both male, so I checked them out in the phone book. One - Alphonse - told me over the phone that he had no relatives named Ronald. I made another note to have Duane double check that. The other - Malcolm, lived nearby, so I stopped at his address. Nobody was home, so I left a note to call me at the police station.

I temporarily put aside Duane's suggestion about synagogues for the time being and concentrated on doctors, especially since I was more comfortable in doctors' offices than in any religious building. I found three family physicians in the neighborhood where Ronald had lived. At each office, the receptionist checked through the files and found no Schlesinger's listed.

Checking yet again with the Visalia Times-Delta, I did manage to find a reference to a Jacob and Lorelei Schlesinger being killed in a car crash on Highway 65 in 1942. No mention of a Ronald, however.

There were two synagogues in Visalia, the one nearest to Ronald's neighborhood, by far, was B'Nai David. I was fortunate enough to be able to speak with Rabbi Abraham Nussbaum, who I thought looked much younger than I imagined a rabbi would be. He did wear a Yamaka, but he was clean-shaven. I finally got lucky. The rabbi had comprehensive, detailed records dating back several decades. They included births, marriages, funerals. and Bar Mitzvahs. The funeral of the Schlesinger's killed in the car crash had been conducted at this synagogue. There were not, however, any Bar Mitzvahs, marriages, or funerals recorded for anyone named Schlesinger from 1943 through 1960. There was, though, a marriage in 1936, between Jacob Schlesinger and Lorelei Kronig, the couple who were killed. Ronald had died at around age 7 in 1949, so these could very well have been his parents. In fact, he might have been a survivor of the accident, though I couldn't confirm it. Unfortunately, the rabbi said they had both died in that crash before he had become a rabbi, and that his father had conducted their funerals. Just to cover all bases, I asked if there had been anything suspicious about the accident. He didn't know of any such suspicions. It wasn't a lot for all the blisters I was getting on my toes, but at least I had two more names for Duane to research. And what had happened to Ronald after his parents' deaths?

I did think it was significant that there was no record of a Bar Mitzvah. If this synagogue conducted a marriage and a funeral for this family, it certainly would have also officiated at a Bar Mitzvah if there were any boys 12 years or older in the family. I decided that, if this was the right family, and I definitely thought it was, then Ronald was probably the only boy in the immediate family. So if Ronnie had any siblings, it was a sister. But finding a grown sister would be a challenge, since she now probably had a different surname. Besides, females very rarely commit serial murders. Of course, there was the case of Aileen Wuornos, who was currently sitting on death row in Florida for her 7 serial killings. But hers were drug-fueled murders of opportunity in the seamy underworld of prostitution. And a few women have been known to kill off two or three husbands in a row. But what I was dealing with was a series of well-planned, targeted homicides. That is almost exclusively a male occupation. The thought did occur to me that some relative other than a sibling of Ronald's could conceivably have been sufficiently outraged to commit these murders, especially if he were mentally fragile in some way. But that was an avenue of last resort, I felt.

Finally, I went back to Redwood High School and, with the help of a couple of student volunteer office workers, compiled a long list of names of male students who had attended Redwood High along with my three victims and Cory Matcher. That amounted to around a thousand names. I spent several hours looking them up in the Visalia phone book. Out of that number, only 47 appeared in the book. I called each of the numbers and made contact with 27 of the former Redwood High School students. I asked each if they remembered any of my four names. Only five of them remembered one or more of them. I made appointments to come to their homes to talk with them. But I was especially interested in one, in particular - Lionel Carmody. Why Lionel? Because he remembered knowing well all four of the "four musketeers."

25

Unfortunately, as it would later turn out, I needed a rest before interviewing Mr. Carmody, so I headed back to the office, where Duane had completed his Lexis-Nexis search. For the most part, it had been unproductive. He had not managed to confirm Ronald's birth date through census records, because the kid hadn't been born yet at the time of the 1940 census. And, since he had been deceased by the time the 1950 census came out, there was nothing there, either.

"So I tried a few other kinds of databases, and his name popped up in the records of something called the JFFSD, a Jewish refugee resettlement organization as being a member of the family of Marvin and Ethel Bronson. Bronson? Not Schlesinger? And no, I don't know what JFFSD stands for. Anyhow, I went forward to the 1950 records and found the Bronson's living at an address on the same street - Stover Street - as the Schlesinger's had lived on Marvin was listed as 39, Ethel 37, and Alicia, 6 - their daughter, I presume. But here was the big surprise. It listed one Ronald Schlesinger, 7, as another resident. Since you said he died in 1949, I thought it odd that he would pop up on a 1950 list. I guess they had not yet had time to update their records since he was killed."

"You're right, Duane. Something's off here. Who, for instance, were the Bronson's? And why was Ronald Schlesinger listed as living with them. But I'm betting we'll find out more about all that as we get closer to solving these murders."

26

Duane, Irma, and I pretty much constitute the entire Oak Hill Police Department, and I realized that my obsession with this case was not furthering the responsibilities of policing my little town. So I took a day off from the investigation and the three of us cleaned up a lot of business. Irma, in particular had been swamped with work for the past several days, what with me gone so much, and I decided that I would get her out of the office for a while. So the next day I left Duane in charge of the routine police work as well as Lexis-Nexis and took Irma with me to visit Lionel Carmody, who had told me on the phone that he had known the musketeers.

Irma Kamimura is a special person. Her grandparents had been unjustly incarcerated during WWII, even though they had become U.S. citizens after coming from Japan to create a farm in this lush agricultural valley. By the time she was born, a lot of that racial animus had dissipated, but not entirely. She attended U.C. Davis, intending first to get a degree in horticulture to honor her grandparents, but switched to criminology after being fascinated by the Manson murders down in L.A. I had been in a patrolman in the LAPD at the time, but not involved in that investigation. She had originally intended to enter law enforcement in my old bailiwick. But Eddie South, the Chief Constable of Oak Hill, used his irrepressible charm to entice her to stay in her hometown and help him. Which she did. It was always hard to say no to Eddie. Irma was in her early 40's at the time, about 5'2". Her smooth, jet black hair is usually worn in a page boy style. And like most Asian women, it seems, she appears ageless. I can only speculate as to why she remained single, so I won't.

I was pumped up to be able to finally talk to Lionel Carmody, the only alumnus of Redwood High I talked to on the phone who claimed to clearly remember the Schlesinger tragedy in any detail, including having known the "Musketeers" pretty well.

We got to Carmody's house at around 7:00 P.M. I knocked on the door but there was no answer. Still, there were lights on in the house and I could hear the TV. So I knocked harder, pounded, then called out his name and mine.

Irma said, "I'll check around back."

Less than a minute later, she returned with a perplexed expression.

"I hate to tell you this, Arnie, but there's a hole cut in the patio door."

This murder was not like the ones that did in three of the musketeers, in that it didn't happen in the victim's bed, late at night. It was more like Tom's murder. The killer had confronted Mr. Carmody in his living room in broad daylight and shot him; nor was there a photo left at the scene, at least not at first sight. There were other differences. The victim was shot in the heart, and not in the head; and it was too far away to have left powder burns, such as were present on the other victims. It was hard to tell, yet, whether it was a break-in, or whether the killer was invited in, killed Mr. Carmody, and faked the patio door break in. The oozing blood suggested that he had just been shot. And this time it was in the daytime, suggesting desperation on the part of the killer. My guess was that he had just found out that Carmody had been contacted by me, and had to act swiftly. Finally, the circle of glass, which lay broken on the threshold had not been taken away.

He had no vital signs, but Irma started immediately administering CPR as I called 911. I stood ready to take over when she got tired. "You know, Irma, we might have just missed the killer."

"Really?"

"Well, even though this man, who I assume for now is - WAS - Lionel Carmody, appears deceased, he is warm and still leaking blood. Irma, we just missed catching this perp in the act. DAMMIT!"

"Oh, I just remembered!", she said

"What?"

"As soon as I came 'round the corner to the back door, I heard a car that sounded like it was laying rubber in the alley."

I ran to the alley with my gun drawn, but saw nothing suspicious, at first. But there was a short, clear stretch of tire tracks.

My head was swimming. Why was Lionel Carmody killed? Was he yet another of the musketeers? That was not likely, since nobody in this case had yet mentioned the existence of a "5th" musketeer. Was the killer somebody who knew I was on my way to question Lionel? But how was that possible? The only people I told were Duane and Irma. There were a couple of other far-out theories that entered my head, then left just as fast, because they seemed preposterous. The best answer I could come up with was that the killer knew somehow that I was closing in and realized that Lionel Carmody was a loose end who knew some vital stuff about the musketeers. And, from what I had already learned, he DID know all four musketeers well. I wanted to kick myself for putting off this visit, because I was pretty sure Lionel Carmody could have provided a key piece of my puzzle. And again, if that was true, the killer was most likely someone whose path I had already crossed and he was fearful of me talking to Mr. Carmody. Besides that, there was the apparent absence, so far, of a photo left at this scene, which suggested to me that either the killer had run out of copies of the photo, or Mr. Carmody, like Tom, was killed, not out of revenge, but out of fear of exposure. Add to that the fact that the murder was carried out in broad daylight, or at least at dusk, I was dealing with someone who may have been super smart, but who was increasingly desperate.

Mr. Carmody was yet another link to the death of a little boy 45 years ago and he was now dead. So the motive for the killings was becoming more and more clear, but the identity of the killer still seemed just out of reach. One thing was very clear, though, Cory Matcher, who was under federal surveillance, as well as the scrutiny of Tulare detectives, did NOT do this particular killing.

Up to now, the preponderance of the evidence had pointed to Cory Matcher, and if anyone knew I was getting close, it was he.

But most detectives with any significant amount of experience get pretty good at sensing whether someone they're questioning is guilty or not. In fact, the majority of murders are solved, not by DNA and fingerprints, but by canny detectives who know in their gut who's guilty, and are experts at eliciting confessions. Eddie used to be able to do it with friendliness and kindness. Not my style. I threaten and instill fear

Well, both my gut and the evidence were telling me that Cory Matcher, while not exactly being Mr. Clean, was no murderer. Either that, or he was one of the smartest I ever encountered. If I was right, someone else I had run into was getting scared. And the only name that came to mind seemed so farfetched that I immediately rejected it.

I called Harry and Bud in Tulare and told them what was happening and to be sure to bring a full forensics team, because, from all appearances, this crime was committed in a big hurry and the chances for physical evidence being left behind was pretty good. Once the first responders arrived and took over from Irma, she joined me in the alley.

"Nothing much here, Irma. But these tire tracks sure look like a car peeled out just like you said. We need to make sure forensics gets molds of the tracks."

While Irma and I waited for the Tulare sheriffs to arrive, we went back inside and watched the EMT's work, These dedicated people always amaze me the way they keep trying to resuscitate somebody they know is dead. I looked around for another copy of the photo of the kid on his tricycle, but I didn't find any. The lack of a photo made me all but certain that Carmody was killed because of what the killer was afraid he would tell me. That's when the thought struck me that if this killer thought Mr. Carmody had already spilled the beans, the perpetrator would probably not stop short of trying to kill me, for the same reason Tom had been targeted. That intrigued and excited me. I could use that desperation to my advantage.

27

The first mistake the killer may have made in his haste to eliminate Mr. Carmody as a threat was to park in soft dirt in the alley, assuming we were right and the reason there was a car peeling out in the alley was that it was being driven by a panicked killer. So, when Harry and Bud arrived, we all walked out to the alley and saw immediately some fresh, distinct, tire prints. They only extended a couple of feet, because, once the car began spinning its wheels, any more prints were obliterated. But that was all right; two feet are as good as a mile when it comes to tire prints. So Harry hurried out to his car to retrieve from his trunk a tire print kit before the sun went down completely. Then he began mixing plaster and pouring it over the tread prints.

"So you think these prints are really from the killer's car, Arnie?"

"Who knows, Harry? But I'm not taking any chances. Besides, take a look around. Can you think of any reason a car would have parked right here? There are no garages or parking spaces along the alley. Whoever parked here WANTED to park right here and nowhere else. And when he left he was in a big hurry. I'd bet my pension that this was the killer's car. Besides, you could still smell the gunpowder inside the house, so the killer had to be close by when we arrived. I'm picturing this perp hearing us knock on the front door right after he shot Carmody, and he hightailed it out the back door just before Irma got around back. So close, dammit! I think we should start looking for footprints, too. If this shooter left as fast as I think, there was no time to erase any prints he might have made in this soft dirt. There's some kind of impressions over there by that bush, but if they are footprints they are blurred, maybe by a plastic bag placed over them."

"Gee, Arnie, I didn't know you were getting a pension for being chief."

"What're you talkin'...oh I see. I'm not, but I do have my LAPD pension. And now that I think about it, I wouldn't bet it, either."

We looked around for readable footprints but found none. So we figured that our quarry was at least smart enough to jump over the patches of dirt while running away. In fact, this was just another piece of evidence suggesting that this was the killer.

Harry, Irma, and I went back into the house as Bud continued looking for evidence in the alley, I went out to my car and got my latex gloves. Before starting my part of the premises search, I stood staring at the corpse for a couple of minutes. There was a lot more blood than at the other murder scenes, and there was a short blood trail, so I assumed Mr. Carmody either tried to flee or to fight his attacker. But if so, it was a short fight; the bullet had hit dead center in the middle of his chest. I decided to start with the most likely place to find evidence, especially since the ATF thought there was a drug connection - the bathroom. I checked the labels of all the pill bottles and lotions, and found nothing suggesting Mr. Carmody was a druggie, legal, or otherwise. When I went to his bedroom, it appeared that it doubled as an office, so I went through everything as thoroughly as I could. One thing I was still looking for, but failed to find was another photo of Ronald on his tricycle. Not that I was surprised that I didn't. Mr. Carmody was apparently not an integral part of the musketeers, so the killer had a different reason for killing him, just as in the case of Tom. I found an old copy of his Redwood High yearbook, and found one photo of him standing and grinning next to Cory Matcher in the advertising section, which lent credence to his claims of at least a tenuous "musketeer" connection.

I was just about to terminate the search when I noticed there was something tucked underneath the blotter pad, so I lifted it and there was a folded copy of the Tulare edition of the San Francisco Chronicle. What intrigued me about it was that Mr. Carmody lived in Visalia. Why was he interested in an out-of-town paper? and interested enough to shove it under his blotter pad? The paper had been opened to some inside pages prior to being folded, which suggested to me that there was something on the two exposed pages of importance to him. Mostly, it was classified ads, with a couple of small ads for local businesses in Tulare.

But I didn't have the chance to examine it more carefully, because I heard a phalanx of vehicles pull up in front of the house; the cavalry had arrived. I thought for a moment I should return the newspaper to its hiding place. But then I figured that, if there was anything of value in this paper, I would be the one most likely to spot it, so I folded it further and stuffed it inside my uniform jacket.

Among those who now showed up was "The Greek Geek." That's what I call Max Axopolis, the 6'8" Tulare County Medical Examiner. Others refer to him as "Max the Ax," or sometimes "Mad Max." In any case, he's a top notch M.E.

"Arnie, good to see you; how long has it been?"

"About a year, when the teachers were killed."

"I didn't see you at any of the other murders the last month."

"They were out of my jurisdiction. And I was out of town when Tom was killed."

"That was a damn rotten shame. This county is going to miss him."

"I haven't heard who might be replacing him."

"Me neither. Hey, Harry, you interested?"

"Hell, no, Max; there'll have to be a special election. You aren't interested are you, Arnie? Pays a lot more than the job you've got, now."

"No, I'm getting too old to be striving upward and onward, I'm looking forward to retirement, again. Besides I've got all the money I'll likely ever need."

"Independently wealthy?"

"No, just cheap."

"I'll vouch for that," said Bud.

While Max knelt down, opened his bag, and started probing

for evidence on and around the body, Bud and three other deputies started their own search of the house.

"Well, Irma and I have to be getting back to the station; Duane's been holding down the fort. Let me know if you find anything interesting, okay?"

"Sure thing, Arnie."

My gut was telling me they weren't going to find anything more interesting than the newspaper I had in my jacket. Other than the likelihood that Carmody was killed by a .22, I guessed.

"Oh, and just like before, we have to get forensics to determine whether he entered through the patio or the front door. If that was his car in the alley, I assume it was through the patio."

28

On the way back to the station, I took a bit of a detour and stopped at the Jiffy-Lube where Cory Matcher worked. His boss confirmed that he'd been working there all day, so I finally had managed to eliminate one potential suspect for this murder, and probably the others, as well. Irma and I spoke with Cory briefly as he was greasing the underside of a car.

"Cory, do you remember a guy in high school named Lionel Carmody?"

"Yeah, why?"

"Because he was just murdered a couple of hours ago."

Cory dropped his grease gun.

"What?!"

"So I just wanted to give you a heads-up. Everybody associated with your old musketeers seems to be a target of this killer, so you be VERY careful. Chances are, this killer is somebody you once knew, so don't take any chance trusting any of them, if you run into them. And I strongly advise you, if you know anything about this you'd better tell us if you expect us to be able to protect you."

Cory just stared at me.

"All right then, see you later, I hope." Irma and I left, but he was visibly shaking.

When we got back to my office, Duane was still at his computer.

"Sorry, Arnie, I've checked a lot of data bases, but nothing else about any Schlesinger's who might have lived in this area."

"Try Alicia Bronson."

"Right, I forgot about her."

"And while you're at it, might as well check all of the victims, as well as Mister Matcher to see if they cross reference in some way with other than the 'four musketeers' or Alicia. I doubt there's anything there, but gotta cover all the bases"

"Will do."

As Duane typed away on the keys of his MacIntosh, I reflected on my resistance to modernity and realized I needed to learn more about the advantages of becoming computer savvy. Then again, maybe not, since I was going to be retired soon, and maybe dead before I learned how to use the computer effectively. So I lay back on the little couch in my office and pulled out the crumpled newspaper - the one I had purloined from Mr. Carmody's desk. I went carefully though all the classified ads. Unfortunately, if one of them had caught Mr. Carmody's attention, he didn't make any marks to indicate it on the pages. This particular page had both want ads and items for sale. None of them rang any bells in my head. Just for the heck of it, I went through the rest of the paper. Nothing was marked; the stories were all standard small-town stuff. At this point, I was feeling pretty weary, so I dropped the paper in my lower desk drawer and closed my eyes for a little nap, which is how I had spent most of my early years in school.

29

"Hey, wake the hell up, Crockashit."

Even before I opened my eyes, I knew who it was, because Arthur Granger - "Laurel" - is the only one who ever called me that.

"Oh hey, Art, what's up?"

"Well, not you, obviously."

"Don't hassle me; I'm an old man who needs his naps. In case you didn't know, there was another murder, earlier today."

"No shit? Who?"

"His name was Lionel Carmody, and he was evidently tight with the other victims when they were at Redwood High School together. back in the fifties"

"Well, I'll be darned. Then what are you doing sleeping here?"

"Not in my jurisdiction. Tulare sheriffs are all over it, though. If it weren't for Tom's murder, I wouldn't be having anything to do with it."

"Well, I thought you might want to get in on this. We got another tip. The caller said that a big load of drugs from Mexico will be coming into the Porterville airport, late tonight. Thought you might want to get in on it"

"Maybe. You think this is the same tipster that implicated Walter Knobb?"

"They tell me the voice sounds the same - kind of muffled."

Duane had stopped typing momentarily to follow the conversation. "Walter Knobb. That's a name I haven't run, yet. I'll do that right now."

"Duane's using his Lexis-Nexis skills to try to find connections between our victims and suspects. That is if I HAD any suspects."

"What about the guy we're watching, Cory Matcher?"

"Well, he might be involved in drugs, though I doubt it; I've never found him any place but at home or work. One thing for sure, though: he has a rock-solid alibi for today's murder, which pretty much knocks him to the bottom of the ladder as a suspect in all the murders as far as I'm concerned."

"Unless there's some kind of cartel pulling off these murders."

"I hadn't thought about that. And I don't intend to spend any time thinking about it in the future."

"Maybe you should," Arthur countered. "Here's the way we're starting to see it: this Knobb dude and Cory Matcher are part of a drug cartel smuggling cocaine from Colombia, according to our tipster. If that is so, maybe these murders are being committed by more than one of their members. That being said, there is the possible connection between Knobb and his killers that Tom ran across inadvertently and..."

"Got it!" said Duane.

"Got what?"

"Walter Knobb's sheet, chief. He's been busted three times for possession; convicted once, for which he did two years at Folsom."

"Really? What about dealing or distributing?"

"It only mentions possession here."

"Well, then, since my investigation has hit a stone wall, maybe I should take a break from that and take a closer look at your leads. After all, when it comes to drugs, you guys are the experts; I'm just a small town hick cop who gives out speeding tickets. Anyway, it might be fun to watch you feds bust some big time drug dealers, especially if any of them could be connected to any of our victims, like Knobb."

After dinner that night, I kissed Marjorie and started putting on my cop paraphernalia.

"See you later, I'll try not to wake you; I expect I'll be home about two or three."

"Where are you going, father?"

"I've got to go to work for a while."

"Gonna catch bad guys?"

"Not exactly, honey; I'm going to watch some other cops catch bad guys over in Porterville."

"Are you going to help them?"

"Not if I can help it."

I drove to the office, where I met up with Laurel & Hardy to hitch a ride to Porterville. It only took about 20 minutes to get to the small airport, which was set out in the middle of alfalfa fields southwest of the town. It had only one landing strip about 5,000 feet long, capable of handling only small planes no larger than twin engine. We sat in the car, flanked by 5 other nondescript cars full of ATF agents, most hidden between the buildings. We were parked in a truck lot at the northern end of the landing strip, where we expected the incoming plane of interest to come to a stop before turning around and taxiing back to the administration building. We were only about a quarter mile from the Sequoia National Forest Headquarters, which, as I would soon discover, was an interesting coincidence. But I digress.

We were waiting for a twin-engine Cessna, number N987AB, to land at 1:15 A.M. So we waited. And waited. And waited. Along about 2:30, it looked like the bust would be just that - a bust.

"A godddamned waste of time," sputtered Myron.

"But it looked so promising. Even the number of the plane," said Art.

"Tell me this," I asked. "Who do you think your tipster was?"

"Darned if I know," said Art.

"Think about it. Whoever called in that tip must have wanted to get as many FBI and ATF agents on a goose chase late at night for what reason?"

"You tell us."

"Let me ask you this: where did all these agents come from?"

"Four of them were sent all the way from D.C. But most were from offices in San Francisco, Fresno, and Bakersfield."

"And what would they have been doing if they hadn't been here."

"A number of things - mostly surveillance, I guess."

"Anything near here?"

"Now that you mention it, there were four agents from the Fresno office stationed near Hume Lake."

"That little lake out in the middle of the Sequoia National Forest?"

"That's the one."

"Why?"

"As I understand it, they had two agents watching each of the only two roads out of the area."

"Again, why?"

"We had an undercover acting like a fisherman jawing with the locals for a couple of weeks because of tips of marijuana being grown there. Most of the people who live there are ultraconservative, anti-government types; some of 'em think growing pot thumbs their noses at the government, which fits comfortably with their own hatred of the feds. He was trying to fit in among the locals and find out exactly where it was, since none of our reconnaissance aircraft spotted any significant places likely for marijuana cultivation."

"I wouldn't think so, what with how thick the forest is around there."

"Yeah, but there are a few commercial flower growers in the area, and apparently one or more of them may have been growing more than flowers."

"But you didn't know which?"

"We would have needed warrants to go in and start tearing up their flower businesses, and we didn't have enough evidence for that."

As usual, Arthur had been doing all the talking, but then Myron chimed in.

"So, then they got the bright idea of just letting them grow all the pot they wanted and catch them trying to transport it out by car, or more likely trucks, on one of the two roads out. There are no places there to land a plane."

"What about one with pontoons landing on the lake?"

"That's what our undercover is watching for. Besides, right now the lake is frozen over."

"Jeez, Myron, in the two and a half years I've known you I don't believe you've ever spoken that many words, total."

"Well, this is pissing me off."

"So, you guys thinking what I'm thinking?"

"That the tip about the airport was meant to draw away agents so they could get their marijuana out, tonight."

"And did it?"

"Unfortunately, we don't know, yet. Not until we debrief our undercover. In any event, it DID pull our surveillance away tonight."

"Somebody figured that, if you guys thought this huge shipment from Mexico was coming in, you'd pull off all your available agents from their other jobs, and come running for this mega-bust."

"Sure looks like it, doesn't it?"

"And I'm guessing that, before you set up this airport bust, your people did some kind of background check on the plane's number to make sure it was the real deal."

"To tell you the truth, Arnie, I don't know."

"I'll bet they did; and I'll bet that the tipster is involved in some way with whatever is going on over at Hume Lake. Well, marijuana lawbreakers don't hold any interest for me, whatsoever. However, I can't help thinking that the fact that Walter Knobb was into pot before he was killed, and the fact that the tipster fingered another one of the old musketeer crew, suggests that maybe there could be some kind of connection between this almost drug bust and the murders, so maybe this wasn't a waste of time. I've got some other leads to follow in this county, but, if nothing surfaces, I might just go fishing at Hume Lake, myself. Who knows, maybe I'll find a lead up there." I didn't say it aloud, but I was thinking, "Flowers, hmmmm."

On my way back home my thoughts intermingled uncomfortably. First of all, Cory Matcher? a big shot drug dealer? I couldn't picture it. Also, how did Violet Strand's murder fit into all of this? Was she in reality a little old lady drug dealer? I hardly thought so. Then there is the matter of the fact that at least three of the victims were shot with the same gun. And if it turns out that Carmody was shot with that gun, as well, that effectively eliminates Matcher for at least four of the murders, and, by extension, some kind of cartel murder spree.

30

The next day, after the debacle in Porterville, I got back into the swing of things by following my own leads, not the ATF's. I didn't make any effort to investigate the latest killing of Mr. Carmody. First of all, the Tulare Sheriff's Department was fully involved and competent in investigating that crime; besides Harry and Bud would keep me up to date as needed. The thing I wanted most to know was whether he was killed with the same gun as the others; though I would have been very surprised if he wasn't.

I was still intrigued by the revelation that someone named Alicia Bronson may have lived in the same home with Ronald Schlesinger at about the time when Ronald was killed. Who was she? Apparently, she was about Ronald's age. She might, of course, have been totally unconnected with any of the crimes I was investigating or the death of Ronald. But I couldn't get her out of my mind; I had to know more about her, especially since she and her apparent relationship to Ronald was the only viable lead I had to follow from the deep past.

So, as before, I went to the B'Nai David Synagogue in Visalia. And - my good luck - they had some of the information for which I was searching. In 1942, a family called the Bronson's applied to adopt a baby placed recently in their Jewish orphans facility. The baby had been orphaned when his parents, the Schlesinger's, were killed in an automobile accident a year earlier. They had previously escaped Hungarian Jewish pogroms in 1939. They had been among the fortunate few Jewish families smuggled out of Europe by the Swedish hero, Raul Wallenberg. The child's name was Ronald.

The Bronson family had also come from Hungary about the

time - 1934 - when Hitler first began to gain power in Germany. They had prospered and owned a property that was rented in 1939 to the newly-arrived Schlesinger's. Both families were members of the B'Nai David Synagogue. Finally, I found that a baby named Alicia was born to the Bronson's about the time Ronald was adopted. So one big piece of the puzzle could now be inserted into the overall puzzle. At the time Ronald was killed, he was likely living with the Bronson Family, and had a quasi-sister named Alicia, about his age.

Of course, all that did not explicitly put me nearer to solving these murders. But my gut feeling was that, in some way, it did. Why, I don't know, but I decided to go back to the Jiffy-Lube and ask Cory Matcher if he remembered anyone named Alicia Bronson. He claimed he didn't; but he did recall delivering newspapers to a house with the name "Bronson" stenciled on the mailbox, and that he often saw a little girl there with Ronald.

"Did you ever talk to her?"

"Not that I recall. She seemed very shy."

"Did you see her at 'Devil's Slide' the day Ronald was killed?"

"I don't remember; that was a long time ago. Anyway, after about a year or so, she always seemed to be avoiding me when I delivered papers. I got the feeling she didn't like me, for some reason." I could think of one possible reason, but i didn't voice it, just now.

As soon as I left Cory, I headed back to - you guessed it - the Redwood High School library. I found her in the '57 yearbook freshman class picture, but not in the '58', '59, or '60 yearbooks. Why not? I assumed she had moved to another high school. I considered going to other valley high schools, but that prospect made me shudder. I was already bleary-eyed from looking through just one yearbook. Anyway, she could have been at any of ten thousand high schools in the U.S. at that time. There had to be ways of using my time more productively.

Checking in again with the synagogue, it appeared that the Bronson's had left the synagogue around 1958. So I assumed the family moved out of the neighborhood served by Redwood High School. I couldn't think of a pressing reason why I should run all over the county. So I figured I'd let Duane try to trace their whereabouts on Lexis-Nexis, while I pursued more promising investigative avenues. Besides, I had promised L&H that I'd follow up on the Hume Lake info, though I was not very optimistic that it would lead anywhere. But at least it was more promising than a 1957 Redwood High School yearbook, at this point.

31

First, though, I decided to finish the day with a return visit to Tom Whiting's fiancé, Laura Duval. It had occurred to me that Tom may have stumbled onto this situation at Lake Hume, and that it might be connected in some way to the murders. Despite her continuing grief over Tom's loss, she graciously invited me in.

"I'm not going to take up any more of your time than necessary, Laura, but did Tom ever mention going over to Lake Hume, recently?"

To my surprise: "Yes, he did. I had forgotten about that. He did say he had reason to believe he could pick up some information up there."

"How long was he there?"

"He went early in the morning and got back for dinner."

"And?"

"And? Oh do you mean did he find out anything?"

"That's right."

"He didn't say so, but I got the impression that he might have; though, if he did, he didn't say anything to me about it."

So, I thanked Laura and headed home for dinner.

As I chowed down on Marjorie's chicken cacciatorre, I casually mentioned that I would be gone for a few days to Lake Hume.

"I assume it's not for fishing."

"Nope, I hate fishing."

"Can I go with you?"

"Sorry, Nancy, but this is business. Besides, you have school. You like school, don't you?"

"Yeah, but this sounds like more fun."

116

"Well, as much as I'd love to have you with me, this could be dangerous. Anyway, you still have a lot of catching up to do because of not going to school until last year."

"I'm pretty smart, though."

"Yes, you are. In fact, you're a lot smarter than I was at your age. I hardly ever studied, so I didn't get to go to college. Your mom and I want you to go, though."

"You didn't go to college, but you still got to be the head policeman of the whole town."

"You think I wanted to spend my life being a policeman? I didn't. There were lot of things I would have liked better; but they all required a college education. I'm not saying I'm sorry I became a cop; but there were a lot of things I would have liked better."

Nancy didn't say anything else, but Marjorie did.

"You know, Arnie, I always thought you were one of the top students at Oak Hill High School."

"That's because most of my friends were not only smart, but they were the smartest in the school, and everyone assumed I was a 'brain', like them. It's not that I was dumb; it was just that I hated school. All I really wanted to do was play. And follow you around."

The next morning, I stopped at our local sporting goods store to get some fishing equipment.

"I didn't know you fished, chief."

"I don't. I just need a few things so I can pretend to be fishing up at Hume Lake, if it doesn't cost too much."

"You know, don't you, that the lake is probably all froze up right now?"

"Maybe so, but maybe I can find one of those places where you can sit inside of a shack on the ice and fish though a hole."

"To each his own, I guess."

"How much would it cost for all the gear I need?"

"Well, I'd give you a good deal, chief, but I'd be glad to lend some used equipment."

"Really? That would be great, thanks."

"Glad to help out any way I can for the man who caught

Eddie's killer. Besides, maybe you'll get to like fishing and buy some equipment for real."

"Not likely; but if I do, you'll be the one I buy it from."

Next, I went directly to Highway 65, then north to 198 in Visalia, then northeast to the 180. A few miles farther as I wound my way up into the Sierras I passed the location of the world famous General Grant tree, the largest Sequoia and the 2nd largest tree in the world. It's well over 100 feet in circumference, almost a football field high, and began its life in biblical times.

But I didn't stop there to sight-see. As it happened, it was also the location of the Grant Grove Cabins, where I could get rustic accommodations for about $30 per night. In fact, these cabins were very similar to where I had happily lived in the San Bernardino mountains for years before coming to Oak Hill. Fancier hotels nearer the lake were well over $100, and, if I hadn't mentioned it before, I am cheap. It was well worth the additional 10 mile drive back and forth to the lake in order to find cabins that cheap. I paid for two nights and wasted no more time getting started.

The 10 mile drive was on a steep, winding, narrow road that climbed up though the Sequoias to Hume Lake, at about 6,000 feet elevation. It was further complicated by snow. One spur road was completely closed to traffic, and this one was narrowed to where it was barely wide enough for two cars to pass.

I made it to the lake a little after 2:00 P.M. and drove to the south end, where there was a semblance of an actual town. You could stand at one end and see the other end. After parking by the lake shore, I walked through what town there was to get the lay of the land. Essentially, the town was two blocks long and a half block wide. There were two real estate offices, a small coffee shop, an antique shop, an auto mechanic's shop, a small grocery store, a small shop that sold fishing gear and bait, and a small barber shop. Everything was, well, small. As I passed a barber shop I decided I needed a haircut. I hadn't had one in a barber shop since the day before I got married, choosing instead to occasionally shear off what little hair I had left before it reached my collar. But I was happy to find one here, because there is no better place to get information in a small town than the barbershop.

There were only two customers besides me - one in the chair and one sitting next to me. They and the barber gave me curious looks, but didn't say anything, so I just picked up a well-worn copy of Field & Stream and pretended to be reading it. The three men carried on a running discourse on politics, religion, and more politics.

Max (in the chair): "Whaddya think? You think that cocksucker Clinton did the nasty with that Gennifer Flowers broad?"

Barber: "Of course, he did; it was on '60 Minutes,' wasn't it?"

Earl (next to me): "I'll believe anything about him. He's a phony, bleeding-heart, liberal, pinko."

Barber: "No doubt about that. 'Course, when she sued the Clintons, the judge dismissed it."

Max: "Of course he did. The Clinton's - 'Slick Willy' and that shrew wife of his run the country. They tell all the judges what to do."

Barber: "The only way they'll get that S.O.B. out of there is if they impeach him."

Earl: "You got that right. What the hell does 'impeach' mean'?"

Max: "It means the Congress votes to kick him out of office."

Barber: "It ain't easy, though. I'm pretty sure they've never been able to do it before."

Earl: "There's an easier way, y'know."

Barber: "What's that?"

Earl: "You know..." He raised his arms like was was aiming a sniper's rifle. It was all I could do to hold my tongue.

It went on like that, covering Clinton, The Gulf War, queers destroying the army, and so forth until the Barber finished with both Max and Earl, during which time I just kept pretending to read my magazine. When it came my turn and I climbed into the chair, Max and Earl didn't leave; they sat down and watched me in silence as the barber grilled me.

"How do you want it, mister...what's your name?"

"Arnie. Oh, I'm not particular; just make it short all around."

"Who was your last barber, anyway?" he asked, as he stood back and appraised me as though he were smelling my fart.

"Don't remember. I mostly cut my own hair. I decided to have it professionally cut, because my daughter has a Christmas party coming up."

"Oh, that explains it. Short all around, huh? You got it. Don't recall seeing you in here, before. New in town?"

"Just came up to check out the fishing."

"Ain't nobody fishing here in December," said Max.

"So I noticed. I thought maybe there would be those ice holes inside of a shack, like I saw on the TV."

"Some, but they're all cut by folks who don't really intend sharing them with anyone, particularly strangers."

"Sorry to hear that. But I also heard about some possible business opportunities, here."

"Here, in this little town?" Earl asked.

"Yeah, my friend, Walter, told me about it a few weeks ago. Says he comes up here on business a lot."

"Walter?"

I noticed that caught the attention of Max and Earl.

The barber joined in. "Walter who, if you don't mind my askin'"

"Walter Knobb, know him?"

"Sounds familiar. You guys?"

"Sounds familiar," said Max and Earl, in tandem."

"Where you from mister?"

"Arnie, please."

"Right, Arnie. Whaddya do?"

"I'm from Oak Hill and I do a little of everything. You might call me an itinerant entrepreneur. Walter seemed to be doing all right, so I thought I'd see what all the fuss is about. Know of any big business opportunities around here?"

"Like what did you have in mind?"

"Oh, you know. Anything I can turn a profit on."

I had their rapt attention. None of them was about to divulge any "business opportunities" that might be available. After all, everybody in town knew the feds had been parking on both roads in and out of Lake Hume; they weren't about to take a chance that I might not be a narc. Actually, the ATF did have an undercover man in town, but I didn't know who. I was pretty sure, though, it wasn't one of these rednecks. If he was, he had a helluva good disguise. I didn't want to give myself away, but I took a chance on pressing a little further.

"I see this is a really small place. I don't see how there could be any big business going on around here."

Earl blurted out, "Well, there's the flower farm."

Max and the Barber swiveled their heads in tandem towards Earl, who looked down at his hands clasped in his lap. He looked like a small child caught fibbing. They just glared at him, and he shrank down and stared at his boots. I pretended not to notice. But I sure did, and it told me I was on the right track.

"Flowers? Really? That's big business?"

The barber decided to play it cool.

"Yeah, we got a pretty big wholesale flower business. They grow'em on a 40 acre plot on the other side of the lake, a piece; then they sell'em to Home Depot, and K-Mart, and them other big stores."

"I might be interested in buying flowers in bulk for re-sale. You think they might be willing to deal with me?"

As Earl and Max looked silently at each other, the barber reluctantly said, "Dunno. You'd have to ask them."

"How do I do that?"

He took a deep breath, looked off through the window, and kind of mumbled, "Just drive up the road there about a mile and you'll see a sign that says "Hume Industries - Flowers". Just take the dirt road a couple miles and you'll come to their offices. They have a big shed there where they sell to local customers. You might be able to buy some."

Clearly, the barber was being very coy. If I was a narc, he didn't want to make the flower farm sound suspicious. By the same token, though, I might be another Walter Knobb, who was in the business of buying marijuana in large amounts, and he didn't want to turn away a potential customer. Besides, if this WAS a pot growing enterprise, I was pretty sure there would be no evidence of it in this retail shed he was sending me to.

32

I followed the barber's directions east from the lake on a rutted, dirt road and came to a large, corrugated metal shed with 3 cars parked in front. I walked inside and saw a variety of flowers in pots displayed on long wooden tables crudely carved out of what appeared to be pine, as well as larger plants in terra cotta tubs alongside the tables. Nothing looked like cannabis plants. There was a lady manning a cash register, and five or so customers roaming up and down the aisles. So I joined them and pretended to be a potential customer. When I got to the last long table of plants, I came to a 12' high, chain-link fence with a heavily padlocked gate guarding the inside. Behind the fence were acres of colorful flowers of all kinds densely packed on long tables. I looked around and could see nothing of interest other than the flowers, themselves. No pot in the pots, so go speak. But, as I turned to leave, I noticed that there was a large metal box just inside the enclosure with "Danger" and a stylized lightning bolt stenciled on its front. Heavily-insulated cables ran from the box to the base of one of the fence posts. The fence was electrified! At night, at least. In addition, it was topped all the way around with barbed wire. They definitely did not want anybody uninvited inside. I picked up a six-pack of zinnias and a flat of ivy, along with a 3 foot long spade and walked to the register to pay. I casually asked the lady if it was possible to get a closer look at the flowers inside the fence. She just said, "No," with no elaboration. I figured that I needed somehow to get inside the flower compound for a closer look; but nobody was going to make it easy for me. I looked down at my newly-acquired spade and started to get a crazy idea.

After I stowed my purchases in the back of my Cherokee, I got behind the wheel and stared at the acres of flowers as I began to plan ways of getting inside that enclosure, which I hoped held pieces that would help me assemble the big picture embedded in this murder puzzle. If it turned out I was wrong, and there was no marijuana to be found, well, at least it was a nice drive in the mountains. That's never a waste of time.

On the one hand, I knew I was getting too old for what I was conjuring up in my mind. On the other, I felt like a kid again, running around playing "guns" in my old neighborhood. Eventually, the kid in me won out.

I drove all the way back to my cabin and plopped myself on the bed to plan in detail what I was going to do next. I decided I had to go back. They say you regret the things in your life that you didn't do, not the ones you did. I didn't eat or drink anything, because I'm an old man plagued with digestive and urinary uncertainties that I didn't want to deal with if I managed to get inside the flower compound.

33

I got back to the north end of the lake right around midnight and parked about half a mile west of town in a spot where my car wouldn't be seen by passersby. Then I worked my way through a forest of sequoias, and a few other pine species I couldn't identify. There was also a carpet of some kind of berries I was forced to trample. I was headed in what seemed to be a southeasterly direction where I reckoned I couldn't miss running into the flower compound. Since the enclosure was a good 200 yards deep east of the pavilion, I could hardly miss it, even in the dark. I soon reached a narrow clearing alongside the likely electrified fence just east of the shed, which was closed with only a couple of low-wattage lights burning inside, along with more serious lighting behind the fence. If there were guards around, I didn't see them. So I took my newly acquired spade and a pair of heavy duty gloves and snuck around behind the shed, up to the metal fence. Clearly, I was not going to be able to climb the fence, barbed wire or not; so I determined that the only possible way in was to dig under it. I started walking along the northern fence line testing the softness of the earth and found a likely spot to dig about half way between the front and rear of the compound. I had dressed heavily and wore molded rubber boots in order to not be grounded should I inadvertently touch the presumably electrically-charged fence. It took me about a half hour to dig a hole under the fence large enough to squeeze under safely.

Once inside, I started walking up and down the aisles of flowers pointing a penlight at the flowers while blocking any stray shafts of light with my free hand. I saw nothing unusual. Nothing, that is, until I got within about 50 yards of the rear of the compound. Now I could see how they were doing it. There were several tables covered with pots of zinnias, and interspersed beneath the colorful blossoms were young marijuana plants. I figured they were nurtured here until they were large enough to sell inconspicuously to customers figuring to grow them further at home. These could not be seen from any distance, including aerial reconnaissance. The pot plants (no pun intended) were scattered among multi-hued flowers that were so brilliant in color that they tended to distract the eyes of any curious folks beyond the fence. I actually found it kind of charming. I really couldn't have cared less if people wanted to avail themselves of a little harmless self-medication, but the ATF was not so sanguine. However, neither they nor any other law enforcement agency could get into the compound without a search warrant. And it appeared that whoever the ATF had planted in town had yet to discover anything to support such a warrant. I had now discovered probable cause. But not for me. I was neither a federal officer nor a Fresno County cop; I had no jurisdiction here. Right now, in fact, I was a wannabe felon. Also, as a rogue law enforcement officer, my illegal entry meant that I couldn't tell any other agencies what I'd found without rendering it useless in court. And if I did get caught, the worst that would happen is that I would lose my job. So what? I was about to retire, anyway. Of course, there was something worse possible; but I didn't want to think about that. But it wasn't as though I had wasted my time. I now had satisfied myself that following the marijuana trail to Walter Knobb and beyond could very well lead me to a killer, which is really all I cared about. So, for the time being, my little secret would remain a secret.

I had started to walk over to my hole under the fence when all the lights came on, flooding the whole compound with intense illumination. I instinctively dropped down on all fours as I heard men hollering something about an alarm being set off. How did I do that? There had to be heat or motion sensors hidden among the plants. I started working my way towards my hole on my hands and knees. Then I heard something that scared the daylights out of me:

DOGS! Several barking dogs had been let loose to find the intruder, so I got up and sprinted for my hole. I squirmed under it as fast as I could and used the spade to partially fill in the hole just as the snarling dobermans tried to dig at it. They also jumped against the fences without being electrocuted, I noticed. They must have turned off the juice to protect themselves against accidental contact with the fence. The men were still about 50 yards back and hadn't seen me, as far as I could tell, so I grabbed the spade and headed into the forest. Fortunately, as old as I was, I could still run like hell, if I needed to.

When I got to my car and started down the mountain, two sets of headlights were closing in behind me. I couldn't drive any faster on the ice-slick road, but neither could they, so I just kept up a steady 30 miles per hour in my 4 wheel drive vehicle. All of a sudden, the lights began fading in the distance. They had broken off the chase, for some reason. Then I realized what the reason was. A black sedan marked "ATF" was parked at the side of the road with two agents inside. They motioned me over, inspected my ID, and shined a light through my interior before letting me proceed. I didn't tell them anything about what I was doing there. I said I made a wrong turn and got lost They said, "Have a good day, sheriff," though it was ptich black out. It was, in fact, starting out to be a pretty good day.

What I had discovered was a unique, if not particularly major marijuana cultivation operation. But that didn't really concern me, because pot was completely off my radar as far as policing my small town was concerned. However, this nocturnal sojourn solidified in my mind that Walter Knobb, and possibly others of the old "musketeers" might have been killed for motives beyond mere revenge. Furthermore, something kept sticking in the back of my mind that made me feel there was an even stronger link between what I had just seen and the murders. I just couldn't quite bring that image into sharp focus, yet. I was getting more pieces for my jigsaw puzzle, but the picture was still cloudy and fragmentary.

34

I knew I wouldn't sleep well in the cabin that night with drug dealers possibly tailing me, so I packed up and left a day earlier than I had planned. I got home early in the morning and managed to slip into the house quietly and went to sleep on the couch.

The next day, I sat at my desk twiddling my thumbs in reverse directions, which not one in a thousand people can do - my claim to fame - trying to decide what to do next. Duane's Lexis-Nexis searches were unproductive, so far; and Harry and Bud had not reported any progress, so I had to come up with something.

All I had was a jigsaw puzzle with lots of pieces, but only a few of them linked up with each other. What I felt I knew for sure was that the killings had something to do with the kid on the tricycle in the photo left at each of the killings. And I knew that at least one of the victims was involved in the marijuana trade.

Another factor kept nagging at me. Was this tipster who managed to draw agents away from Hume Lake with a phony tip the same one who put them on to Cory Matcher's alleged involvement in drug dealing? and if so, why? The fact that Matcher had been a "musketeer," seemed way too coincidental not to be connected in some way.

Since the only thing I had that I was sure of, evidence-wise, was the death of the kid on the tricycle in 1949; that HAD to be at least part of the motive. As for the Marijuana connection, that was too speculative at this point; and anyway, competent federal agents were on that. And Harry and Bud were good detectives who would surely find physical and hopefully forensic evidence illuminating the deaths of Strand, Knobb, Tom, and now, Lionel Carmody. That left me with being the only investigator focusing on the pasts of the victims, so I decided that's what I had to keep doing.

This kid had been killed going down a steep hill on a bicycle. Three people who had been his neighbors long ago had now been murdered. The logical conclusion, as far as I was concerned, was that they had been present at Ronald's tragic, accidental death. A fourth person, Lionel Carmody, who may or may not have been present, nonetheless appeared to have knowledge of the circumstances surrounding all these killings, and he had also been killed, almost in front of my eyes and Irma's. And the remaining member of the "musketeers," Cory Matcher, had been ratted out to the cops as a drug dealer. Was that because he was the only one of the intended victims the killer found too difficult to get to, since he had a wife who was always nearby? So maybe he decided that the next best thing to killing him was to pin the murders on him. That would be risky, though, because it might inadvertently uncover evidence implicating at himself or herself. Yes, I was beginning to think "her". But the nature of the crimes themselves suggested that the perp is not averse to physical risk, so I still leaned toward a male killer.

All of this suggested to me that whoever had been committing these murders also was involved to some extent with Marijuana trafficking in Tulare County. So who could that be? Who could possibly fit a description like that? It had to be somebody very clever, very careful, and very determined. That determination could work against me or for me. It meant that the killer might not be done with his evil work; but it also meant that he might be vulnerable to manipulation or forced to make a mistake.

If the killer had been seething for 44 years over this kid's death, it meant two things: he was someone close to the kid - a friend or relative. It also meant that, in all likelihood, he had maintained some kind of contact with those he felt were involved in the kid's death; he even might have befriended them. I decided to pay Harry and Bud a visit to see what they had learned about Violet Strand and Walter Knobb.

Just then, Irma came in and handed me a fax that had come in the previous day from Phoenix Homicide. It provided a bit more detail about the victim there, Gordon Prospero. There wasn't much of interest except that he had a minor rap sheet for drug dealing. A small piece of the puzzle perhaps, but every piece counts; every piece makes the picture just a little bit clearer. I faxed back to Phoenix detectives a request that they check his phone records, especially any phone calls made in the last year or so to Tulare County area codes 209, 559, 661, and 805; and if so, exactly what were those numbers? It had occurred to me that, if the killer was also involved with drug dealing in some way in Tulare County, the killer's phone number must be in one of those area codes. That's tens of thousands of phone numbers, but there are ways of winnowing them down, especially through the three-digit prefixes. For example, if I took the prefix of one of the victims and scanned the lists for other numbers with the same prefix, a list of persons of interest might be generated; I might have another puzzle piece, however small, to fit into my panorama. For example, everyone who lives in Oak Hill has the same prefix as I do - 264. Also, area code 559 covers the part of Fresno County, wherein Hume Lake is located. So let's say I turned up the fact that someone with the same prefix as one or more of the victims had also phoned Hume Lake; well, I might have something to take a closer look at. Of course, the killer might live far from the victims, but I doubted it. This killer had obviously lived in this area in the past, and would be far more likely to be constantly reminded of Ronald's killing by continuing to live in the vicinity of his murderers.

I had a theory - well not a theory so much as a hypothesis; well, not so much a hypothesis as a conjecture: suppose the killer had been following these people for years, realized that some of them were involved with drugs, and ingratiated himself with them by joining their enterprise to gain more information and their trust. That might create a link to Hume Lake and drug dealing. It was a stretch, I'll admit, but, as I said, it made more sense than anything else I could think of.

There was one possible alternate theory. Maybe none of these killings had anything to do with revenge. What if it had been internecine warfare amongst drug dealers? Maybe the clues pointing to revenge were nothing but a red herring to throw detectives off the drug trail. The biggest problem with that idea, though, was the photo. How would the killer get hold of that old photo unless he had been intimately involved with his victims many years earlier? There was also the extreme unlikelihood that Violet Strand, that ostensibly reclusive, sweet lady was mixed up with drug dealers. I pretty much dismissed that lead as likely a blind alley But I planned, when I had time, to look into her activities a bit more closely.

35

I decided to go back to the beginning, by which I mean 1949, when Ronald Schlesinger was killed. I felt that it was necessary to understand the details behind his death. So who could provide me with those details? First and foremost were Ronald's family members or friends. But the only family members I was sure existed at the time were the Bronson's, who are most likely deceased, and their daughter, who may or not be deceased, as well. How hard would it be to find her, assuming she is alive? Then I remembered Malcolm Schlesinger. He was the Schlesinger I found listed in the phone book but was not home when I went to see him. So I tried calling him again and he answered.

"Hello."

"Hello, is this Mister Schlesinger?"

"Yes."

"Malcolm Schlesinger?"

"Yes it is, and you are..."

"Mister Schlesinger, this is Chief Constable Crockett of the Oak Hill Police Department. I'm looking into some recent homicides in this area and the name of Ronald Schlesinger came up as a young boy who was killed in an accident back in 1949; is there any chance you might be related to him?"

There were several moments of silence during which I could hear him take a deep, wheezy breath.

"He was my first cousin, and it wasn't an accident."

Whoa! A brand new person of interest, perhaps?

"Would it be okay if I came to your house to talk with you about what happened?"

He was reluctant, at first, but seemed to be growing almost eager to talk about something that had been eating at him for 44 years. On the drive over to Visalia, it occurred to me that I might have accidentally uncovered the murderer. Sure, he was willing to talk with me, but he could still be the murderer and simply wanted to vent his anger and frustration over his cousin's death. He might even have wanted to lure me to his house to...you know. My gut feeling though, was that he was not my killer, who I figured was way too clever and devious to expose himself like this. But just in case, I wore my gun and holster, which I don't usually do, even on the job. I did not intend to be caught off guard the way Tom was.

When I reached his house, I was met by a man who appeared to be my age. He was, like me, bald, but unlike me, he had a rather prominent paunch. His skin was pale white and his face deeply wrinkled. I soon found out why. He was a chain smoker. He sat on the couch and offered me a seat next to him. I casually sidled over to an armchair and sat down without comment; all my life I've found it very uncomfortable and disgusting to be near smokers. He seemed to sense it but ignored it.

"Well, chief...Crockett is it?...I'm amazed that, after all these years, somebody in law enforcement has finally gotten around to investigating Ronnie's death."

"Strictly speaking, sir, it's not his death we have been investigating; his name came up in connection with the recent murders of three people in this town."

"You must mean Violet and Walter."

"And Chief Whiting."

"Really?"

"If you don't mind my asking, exactly how are you related to Ronald?"

"He was my father's brother's - Jacob's - son."

"Jacob Schlesinger was your uncle? so Ronald was your cousin?"

"Yes, he was. He and my father came to this country as part of the group of Jews that were rescued by Raoul Wallenberg, a truly great man."

"Yes, I read about him. It must have taken a lot of compassion and courage to do what he did."

"It certainly did; and what was his reward? the Soviet Communists took him away, never to be heard from again."

"I've been to the local synagogue a couple of times learning about Jacob, but your name never came up."

"That's because I'm what you call a secular Jew; I rarely go to synagogue except for special ceremonies. Jacob was very much an observant Jew, however."

"Mister Schlesinger, you said on the phone that Ronald's death wasn't an accident. Could you tell me more about that?"

"He was murdered by a bunch of sadistic bullies."

"By any chance, are you referring to the 'musketeers'?"

"Oh, you know about them, do you?"

"Yes, Violet Strand, Walter Knobb, and Gordon Prospero, who lived in Phoenix, were all murdered.

"Oh, Gordy got it, too? I didn't know about that, but I'm glad to hear it."

"The fourth member of their group..."

"Cory Matcher."

"Right, Cory Matcher told me about the musketeers. We have him under close surveillance, in case the killer tries to go after him, too." I wanted Malcolm, in case he was the killer, to think twice about that. "Pardon my bluntness, sir, but you didn't kill them, did you?"

"WHAT? No, I wouldn't have the guts to do something like that. Wish I did, though. You know, when I read about Violet and Walter being killed, I thought 'Good riddance!' but it never occurred to me that it had anything to do with Ronnie."

"How about Lionel Carmody"?

"Who?"

"Lionel Carmody - one of the murder victims. Was he there, too?"

"I don't know who that is."

I decided to catch him by surprise and gauge his reaction; I pulled out the photo of Ronald on his tricycle when he was about 5 or 6. "Do you recognize this photo?"

He looked at it a bit curiously, at first, then asked, "Is that my cousin?"

"As far as we know, yes, but only one person has actually identified him. What do YOU think?"

"Well, I can't be absolutely sure, but it sure looks like I remember him when we were kids."

As we talked, I watched his expression carefully. He never gave a hint that he was shocked that I had the photo. He didn't strike me as a guilty man. But I've been fooled before.

"Well, sir, I'm not accusing you of anything, but I hope you can account for your whereabouts on the days the killings took place." I gave him all the dates.

"To tell you the truth, chief, I'd have to think hard about that. You see, I'm retired and don't have a set schedule where I see many people. I shouldn't have any trouble, though, proving I wasn't in Phoenix when Gordy was killed."

"I hope so. I'll get back to you in a couple of days about those dates. For now, though, what can you tell me about how Ronald was killed?"

He didn't hesitate. He launched into a detailed description of what took place at "Devil's Slide," in 1949.

As they often did, about a dozen kids from Goshen Elementary School and Divisadero Junior High School had gathered at the top of "Devil's Slide" to coast on their bikes down the frighteningly steep hill. Ronald came along walking a new bike that he was just learning to ride; he was only seven years old. He walked over to the top of the hill to watch, when first one, then several of the clique from Divisadero - eighth graders, he thought - calling themselves "The Musketeers" started teasing him and daring him to ride his new bike down the hill. Ronald backed away, saying "No, not me."

Then the teasing evolved into taunting, but he still demurred.

Finally, one of them said, "Let's put him on the bike and make him go down the hill."

Ronald was really frightened now, and started to leave. But they grabbed him and forced him onto his bike. With two of them holding him in his seat the other two grabbing his handlebars, they wheeled his bike to the edge of the hill and gave it a big push. Ronald screamed and tried to hold on as tight as he could. He couldn't get off the bike, because it was going too fast. The kids at the top laughed, especially the musketeers, as he went hurtling down the hill at tremendous speed. The kids who regularly plummeted down the "Slide" knew, of course, that they were pretty safe as long as they kept their wheels straight, because centripetal force kept their wheels straight and their bikes upright. But Ronald had only just begun learning to ride, and when his panic kicked in, he pulled too hard on one side of the handlebars and forced his wheel to turn just enough to cause the bike to flip and careen completely out of control. In about four seconds - four terrifying seconds - the bike tumbled, cartwheeled and bounced on down the hill, leaving Ronald crumpled in agony about halfway down. All the kids, including the brave musketeers ran away as fast as they could. By the time an ambulance arrived Ronald was dead.

"That's a horrible story, Mister Schlesinger. You ran away, too?"

"I wasn't there."

"Then how do you know all these details?"

"My other cousin - cousin-in-law told me."

"Are you talking about Alicia?"

"That's right?"

"Alicia Bronson?"

"Right."

"You don't by any chance know where she is now, do you?"

"No, I'm sorry. I had never gotten used to her being a part of the family, and she got married right after high school and moved away."

"And I'm guessing you don't know what her married name was."

"Nope, sorry."

36

After I returned to my office, I sat at my desk staring into space; I couldn't get that horrific image out of my mind of that poor, terrified, little kid plunging to his painful, premature death. For the first time, I could understand why someone might have held on to the same image for all those years, dreaming of revenge. It also hit me that I was now investigating, not five murders, but six, including that of innocent, little Ron Schlesinger. Of course, three of Ronald's killers had paid for their crime with their own lives, so far. But any moral revenge that might have underlied an excuse for those killings didn't entitle the avenger to murder Tom Whiting and Lionel Carmody, neither of whom was guilty of what happened to Ronald.

When I got back to my office, I felt moved to get out my photo of Ronald, smiling as he sat on his tricycle, unaware of his impending fate. I stared at it as though some inspiration would jump out at me. It didn't. But it gradually dawned on me that I was holding the one and only piece of physical evidence in this case, and there must be some way I could use it to move forward.

Suddenly, I slapped my forehead and asked myself aloud, "Why didn't I think of that before?" I opened my desk drawer and pulled out the other copy of the picture and studied them both. I had previously speculated that one of these pictures was an original from nearly 50 years ago, while the other was a copy. And, according to Phoenix detectives, the photo they found appeared to be a 2nd generation print, also. No photo was left at the scene of Lionel Carmody's murder, maybe because he hadn't directly participated in Ronald's killing. Besides, the killer probably had to leave in a hurry when Irma and

I knocked on the door. What I hadn't given sufficient thought to previously was when these copies were made. Logic dictated that it was probably recently. What reason would anybody have for making all those copies except to leave them at the murder scenes? It also struck me, for the first time, that there was probably at least one other copy out there: for the fourth likely musketeer - Cory Matcher - and that one must still be in the possession of the killer. If I ever got a chance to get a search warrant for a suspect's property, there was a good chance I would find that photo and see it eventually presented to a jury as evidence.

So, how were these copies made in the first place? There was a possibility that the killer happened to have expertise in film developing; but I thought it much more likely that he took it to a professional at some local film processing shop in Visalia. I got out my yellow pages and quickly found two such shops in town. So I drove to Visalia and stopped at each shop. Unfortunately, the owners said they rarely get requests to make multiple copies of photographs from prints and weren't set up to do so; most people who want multiple copies usually have negatives. It was very unlikely that this killer had been carrying around negatives for all those years. - possible but not probable.

Striking out at the two shops in Visalia, I checked the yellow pages again for shops in Tulare. It turned out there was only one, so I drove 7 miles south to Tulare, and entered the local Fotomat. I showed the proprietor my two photos and he agreed with me that the one with the crinkly edges likely came from an old Kodak photo mini-book, and that the other was a copy. He further confirmed my supposition that this photocopy was made from a print, not a negative. I asked him if he made those kinds of copies, and he said he did but rarely, and that if he had made this copy he would remember, but he hadn't. So, he was certain that he, himself, had not made the one I brought him, but thought that one of his employees might have. He had one such employee in the shop now and checked with her, but she, too, said she hadn't made the copy. There were two other employees not working that day, so the proprietor told me he would check with them as soon as they came to work in a day or two and call me with what he learned. I was disappointed that this avenue of investigation was temporarily stymied, but I left hopeful that it was not yet a dead end.

The other piece of evidence that still existed from the original crime was named Cory Matcher. It was getting to be closing time at the Jiffy-Lube, so I called Marjorie to say I would be late for dinner, and I headed out for Cory's home.

37

Cory was not happy to see me standing on his porch when he peeked though the curtains; he opened the door, but he didn't immediately invite me in.

"Mister Matcher, I have some very important information to share with you about these murders and the danger you're in."

"Danger" was the "abracadabra".

"Come in, please."

After we both sat down, with Cory's wife remaining standing, I said, "Mister Matcher, what I have to discus with you is highly personal, so if you'd rather..."

"It's okay, Marie and I have no secrets from each other."

"It's about the death of Ronald Schlesinger."

"That's all right, I told her; I'd rather she stay."

"It's up to you. Cory, there are two things I must talk to you about. First of all, I very strongly suspect that you are the next intended victim of this killer. So, if you have any idea who it might be, it's vital to you that you tell me."

"Believe me, if I knew, I would tell you; I'm looking over my shoulder twenty four hours a day, seven days a week."

"But you have no idea who might be there?"

"That's right."

"Okay, I believe you, but I need to tell you what I was told this morning by someone who claims to know exactly what happened that day at 'Devil's Slide'."

"What did he say?"

"How do you know it was a 'he'?"

"I don't, I just sort of assumed."

At that moment, I realized that I had perhaps been assuming too much, myself, about the gender of the assailant; but I saved that rumination for later. I proceeded to provide all the detail that I had heard from Malcolm Schlesinger, though I didn't tell Cory his name. All through my description, Cory hung his head and covered his eyes, as his wife folded her arms and shed a few tears as she, too, hung her head. I put heavy emphasis on the terror and helplessness little Ronald must have felt as he was pushed down the hill.

"Look, Cory, I have good reason to believe you were one of the four who held Ronald on that bike and pushed him to his death." I waited for an indignant denial, but he just kept silently hanging his head and covering his eyes.

"If you were one of those boys who made this terrible mistake, you need to tell me, because it will help me find out just who is probably looking to kill you, when he...or she... gets the chance."

Finally, Cory looked up and said, "Look, chief, just suppose I might have been one of the ones who did it, like you think? I know there's no statue of limitations on murder..."

"You mean 'statute.' Look, Cory, as much as I deplore what was done to Ronald, I have no intention of trying to make a legal case for murder against someone who was only a boy of fourteen..."

"Thirteen."

"Thirteen, at the time. I can't guarantee what the Tulare County Sheriff's Department might do, but, given that their focus is on who killed Sheriff Whiting, I doubt very much that they have any desire to punish anyone for the forty five year old indiscretion of some rowdy, thoughtless teenagers."

Marie finally spoke up. "Cory, honey, you have to tell him. You can't go on like this; it's killing you."

Cory looked at her for several seconds, then at me, took a deep breath and told his version of what happened.

"Me an' Walt, an' Gordy, an' Vi had all been drinkin' and having fun flying down the hill and trudging back up. Then this little kid from Goshen came walking up pushing his bike and asked what we were doing. We told him how much fun it was and that he ought to try it. He said he didn't want to, so, stupid jerks that we were, we started teasing him. At some point, everything got out of hand and when he tried to run away, we caught him and forced him to sit on the bike acting like we were going to make him go down the hill. I'm telling you the truth that I never once thought of really doing it, but before I knew it, there he was shooting down the hill screaming. I can tell you that the most horrible thing I've ever seen in my life was when that poor kid went flyin' off his bike and we could see his body bouncin' around like a rag doll, and I just knew he was getting his arms and legs busted. But none of us had he guts to go down and help him. We just took off running - us four and some other kids who had been watching."

He and Marie both started crying uncontrollably. When they calmed down, I asked,

"Do you know if anybody was with Ronald, like a friend or relative?" Or is there any chance you know the names of any of those other kids?"

"Why? Do you think it's one of them that wants to kill me?"

"I have no idea, it's possible. Besides, the more actual eyewitnesses I can contact, the better chance I have of getting an idea of who it is that might want revenge so badly that he is hunting down Ronald's killers all these years later."

"I'm sorry. I don't have any idea who else was there besides us four."

"Is there any possibility that these other kids were threatened not to tell by you and your friends?"

"Not by me. I can't speak for Walt and Gordy, though, they were the rough guys in our crowd."

"Tell me this: did you know any of Ronald's friends or family I could contact if they're still around?"

"No, sorry I don't. The kid was just one of the younger kids from the elementary school, and we never had anything to do with them as best as I can recall. I didn't even know the kid's name till it got in the papers."

"There's one more thing; and again, I have no interest in persecuting you; there are some, especially in the ATF who think that maybe whoever is after you is really angry because of a drug deal gone bad. Is that a possibility?"

"Uhhhh..."

"Cory, I'm telling you, unless you're some kind of big time drug lord, which I seriously doubt, I'm not going to bust you for drugs; I'm only interested in solving these murders and saving your life. So, tell me the truth, are you into drugs of any kind?"

"I smoke a little pot, but I never buy more than a few dime bags, and I always pay cash, up front."

"That's pretty much what I thought, and I think the feds are wasting their time watching you."

"Me? Why would they be watching me?"

I suddenly realized I had opened my big mouth and spilled some beans better left in the can. But I pressed on.

"As I understand it, they got a tip from someone. And my bet is that this someone is our murderer. He is having trouble ever finding you alone like he did the others, so he's either trying to get his revenge by hanging a drug rap on you, or he thinks you'll panic and make a mistake that enables him to get a chance to kill you. So you've got to keep being very careful to not ever be alone, if you can help it."

"You can count on it!"

"Well, thanks for your honesty and cooperation. I want you to know I'm doing my best to get this guy before he gets you. As for punishment for what you foolishly did when you were a kid, I think you are paying for it right now."

"Yes, I think you're right. And I think I deserve it."

"Oh, one more thing: can you tell me who you bought your pot from."

Cory hesitated.

Marie said, "TELL HIM!"

"Walt Knobb."

Now THAT was interesting, but, as it turned out, it wasn't the last piece of interesting information Cory would give me. As I turned to leave, he said,

"Hey, I just remembered. There was one other kid I knew who was at the hill when the kid died. His name was Lionel Carmody, who was a guy I knew at Divisadero. But he wasn't with us."

Now I was pretty sure I knew why Mr. Carmody was killed. I suspected that he saw something in that paper he was hiding that may have triggered a memory and prompted him to investigate, and perhaps do a little blackmailing. It was pure speculation, but it was a piece that fit into my slowly evolving puzzle.

38

On the drive back to the station, I tried to put everything I had so far together - make more of the puzzle pieces fit together. I was not happy that I had so little physical evidence to look at in this case. There were the photos, of course and...well, that was about it, except maybe a few shards of glass left from the break-ins and tire prints. But Bud and Harry would follow that lead. Then I realized that, thanks to Cory's sudden recollection, there was one other piece of physical evidence that I hadn't yet fully examined: that newspaper that seemed to have been hidden by our last victim, Lionel Carmody, shortly before he was killed. I had studied it and found nothing, but I still had a feeling that I had missed something.

The first thing I did when I got back to my office was pull out that newspaper, and I continued staring from where I had left off before. Then it struck me that I should check the date; so I unfolded it to the front page and, sure enough, the date was several days prior to the killing. Why was a copy of this several-days-old newspaper being secreted under the blotter pad on Carmody's desk? Then it occurred to me that maybe he was expecting a visit from someone - his blackmail victim, perhaps? and had hidden it before he arrived. That was reaching a little, I realized, but, hey, it was at least as logical as any other explanation I could come up with.

I re-folded the paper exactly as I had found it and again scanned through the classified ads - mostly "employment opportunities," but I still couldn't gain any inspiration from any of them. Then the word "flowers" caught my eye. But it was not in the classifieds, it was in the paid ads at the bottom of the page. I hadn't paid any attention to them before, but now I looked at them carefully and got a big surprise. One of the ads was for the "Promises Floral Emporium" in Tulare. I wanted to kick myself for not noticing it before. Flowers. The big, secret, marijuana farm east of Hume Lake was masquerading as a flower wholesaler. What if the "Flower Emporium" was a clearing house for marijuana distribution in this part of the San Joaquin Valley? It certainly was a piece that might fit the puzzle. Not only was there the flower connection, but one of the victims - Violet Strand - had worked there when she was killed. At the very least, it needed to be checked out.

Right away, I called the Tulare Sheriff's Department and got hold of Detective Harry Benoit.

"Hey, Harry, we need to get together as soon as possible; I might have some stuff you can use in your investigation of the Knobb and Strand killings. I can be there in about an hour, if you're available."

"Don't bother, Arnie. We were just about to pay a visit to a suspect whose name came up from a phone tip. He lives on the southern edge of Oak Hill, and we'll be going right by your office on the way."

"Let me guess. Cory Matcher."

"Bingo, Arnie."

"And you got a tip on the phone?"

"Like I said, Sherlock."

"Harry, I think this is starting to come together, I'll be waiting here on pins and needles. Bud coming with you?"

"What are you, psychic?"

When Harry and Bud arrived, we hunkered down in my office and started exchanging what information we had accumulated so far. First, they told me that they had examined every facet of Violet Strand's life and found nothing but a young woman named Violet Conklin who had graduated from Redwood High School in 1953, and had immediately married her high school sweetheart, Bruce Strand, who later became a veterinarian. He died of a stroke in 1987, and ever since then, Violet had been pretty much a recluse who rarely left home.

I asked Harry if she'd ever had a job.

"Not that we know of. Her husband left her fairly well-off, so she didn't have to work."

"And yet, right before she was killed she was making a 15 mile round trip to Tulare from Visalia every day to work part time in a flower shop. Doesn't that sound little off, to you?"

"Maybe, but I don't know how it might be important."

"Me neither, just saying."

"Mr. Knobb, though, was a different can-o-worms. He has a long record of petty misdemeanors and a couple of felonies. Never spent much time locked up, though. But his sheet shows that he was involved in drugs, off and on."

"Which gives you another reason to get a search warrant, since he has been known to hang out at Hume Lake, where the feds also suspect something is going on, drug-wise."

"One other thing," said Harry. Turns out Knobb's house had a doggie door, and it was locked when we were there. The neighbors said he had a big German Shepherd, and it was mean. Also, he had a large 'Beware of Dog' sign out front.

"Not only that," added Bud, "the dog was apparently at the vet's recovering from some kind of operation that night."

"Interesting. So the killer just happened to pick the one night the dog wasn't around? That suggests the killer might have known Knobb very well, doesn't it?

"Exactly what we thought," said Harry, "Helps narrow down the suspect list."

Harry and Bud didn't have much else to tell me, so I took my turn. I started out with my excursion to Hume Lake.

"I didn't tell you guys about this before, because I wasn't sure it had any connection to the murders. But Arthur Granger..."

"The ATF guy?"

"Yeah, he told me about Cory Matcher maybe being into dealing drugs. So I went with a bunch of ATF guys on a bust of a plane that was coming into the Porterville airport late the other night, according to a phone tip they had gotten. It turned out that it was a bust in the sense that there was nothing to it. That's when they mentioned that, in order to make this big arrest, they had to pull off surveillance that night on Hume Lake, where they suspected some kind of drug activity."

"Hume Lake? That town up in the Sequoias that thinks Clinton should be impeached and Reagan should be on Mt. Rushmore?"

"That's the one. Anyway, I thought that, since one of my murder suspects, Cory Matcher, was linked in some way to a big drug operation, I thought I'd go there and check it out. My first stop was the barber shop..."

"I thought you were looking unusually spiffy."

"Very funny, Bud. Anyway, the locals were talkative about everything political, but they seemed very hinky when I brought up the name, "Walter Knobb.""

"Knobb? Really?"

"Yep, and that's when they started wondering whether I was a customer or a fed, it seemed to me, so I clammed up. But I went the extra mile and did some surveillance of my own late last night. I can't give you the details, because it might implicate you in extracurricular activities of mine that might not have been strictly legal. Suffice it to say, though: they grow a lot of pot in pots up there, poetry unintended."

"But you don't want to give us any more detail?"

"Trust me, the less you know, the better it will be for any future actions you might take, legally speaking."

"Yeah, maybe you're right."

"Anyway, I humbly suggest that you and the ATF get together and try to come up with an excuse to raid the place."

"And without your info, what would be our probable cause?"

"Well, you are investigating Walter Knobb's murder. And you can use my testimony that some mouthy yahoos at the barber shop seemed to know about him."

"Yeah, maybe, but that's not much to talk a judge into it. Worth a try. The ATF might help by telling the judge about their suspicions based on that tip they got."

"Speaking of which, you guys, just what did your tipster tell you?"

"Not a lot, except that he thought he might be the one who killed Tom."

"'He' meaning Matcher."

"Right."

"Well, I guess you have to check it out, then. But I've questioned him at length three times, and I'm pretty sure he had nothing to do with it, and can prove it."

"Why were you questioning him?"

"I spotted a picture of him in a high school yearbook hanging out with three of our victims. I don't know if the feds are still surveilling him; but take my word for it: they would be wasting their time, though I hope they are keeping an eye on him, because it might keep Mister Matcher from getting killed. But there is one thing he is guilty of, and he admitted it to me a couple of hours ago. He was involved in the unintentional killing of the kid we saw in those photos you found at the crime scenes."

"You're kidding."

"Nope, not at all. The kid in the picture was named Ronald Schlesinger and he was killed a couple years or so after that picture was taken. Everything points to that accidental death back in 1949 as being the motive for the killings that are happening, now."

"I'll be damned."

"Sorry I didn't give you all this before now, Harry, but I thought it was best to let you guys follow your leads with regard to Strand and Knobb, while I followed up on the photo." That way, if one of us was barking up the wrong tree, maybe the other was getting somewhere.

"Anything else you've been holding out on?"

"Well, since you ask, there is one little thing. At the scene of the Carmody killing, while I was waiting for you guys to show up, I found a newspaper that looked like he had been hiding it, and, well, I took it without telling you. I was sure then, as I am now, that it had no forensic value; and I thought it might mean more to me than to you."

"And does it?"

"Maybe so. I just found out that Mister Carmody had witnessed the killing of the kid. And there is an ad in that paper, right where he had been reading, for the Promises Emporium Flower Shop over in your neck of the woods - Tulare.

"We know about that; Violet Strand worked there. We interviewed the lady who owns the shop - Missus Linderman, I think it was. She's the one who reported Strand missing."

"Yeah, I talked to her, also. She seemed nice enough, and cooperative. I didn't learn anything interesting from her, though."

"Naw, neither did we."

"Anyway, I thought that the three way connection: Strand, flowers, and the pot farm at Hume Lake were kind of coincidental."

"And you don't like coincidences."

"Well, I know this isn't a strong coincidence, but it's something I don't think should be ignored. I think you ought to try to get somebody to sort of check it out - you know - sub rosa."

"Hume Lake"?

"No, the flower shop."

"I'm not sure we have anybody we can spare for undercover, right now."

"Well, I might have. I can't do it because Missus Linderman knows me, but...Duane, come in here!"

39

"Hey, Duane, you're always complaining about not having enough excitement in this job; how would you like to go undercover?"

"Cool. When do I start?"

"Tomorrow morning."

"Cool. What do I do?"

"I want you to go buy your girl friend at the Porterville Recorder some flowers."

"Daphne?"

"Yeah. Don't you think she would like for you to buy her some flowers?"

"Probably. Who's paying for them?"

"The City of Oak Hill."

"Really? And why would the city do that?"

"Because you would be performing a valuable service for the community."

"By giving Daphne some flowers?"

"Well, not exactly. I want you to spend every day for the next few days pretending to be a customer of a flower shop in Tulare, so infatuated with your true love that you want to buy her flowers every day. You know, maybe because it's almost Christmas."

"Let me guess. It's that flower shop where Violet Strand used to work."

"That's why you're going to make a great Chief Constable, so I can retire for real."

"So what'll I be trying to find out?"

"First, I want you, being the naturally friendly, attractive, young guy you are, to try to get friendly with Missus Linderman, the owner; I'd like to get a better idea of just who she is."

"Is that all? That doesn't sound like very exciting undercover work to me."

"No, but that isn't all. We think that her flower shop may be a place where major drug shipments come in and are picked up by local dealers."

"That's more like it. Any idea what I'm looking for, in particular?"

"Well, Im guessing that if large shipments are being delivered there they would likely be in trucks or large vans of some kind. They could deliver in the middle of the night, I suppose; but if anybody ever spotted them, it would look very suspicious. I think they're more likely to disguise the shipment as a normal, large, wholesale flower delivery. I'm hoping that you can gain enough confidence from Missus Linderman that she won't notice that, instead of just being a lovestruck young guy, you're actually watching for anything out of the ordinary."

"So I'm supposed to be watching for a large delivery of flowers?"

"That's right. And if the truck or van doing the delivering has 'Lake Hume' or 'Hume Flowers' or anything like that on it, we want to know right away," because it will help us get a search warrant.

"Anything else?"

"Yes. If you notice any suspicious customers - you know the type - who are picking up closed packages, try to memorize their descriptions, or even the names they give, if possible. And If you can tell how much money is being exchanged, or if any kinds of receipts are being put away."

"And then maybe they'll throw them away in the trash bin in the back."

"Good thinking, deputy. Stuff left in trash is legally public property and if we do find marijuana remnants there, it's all we need for a warrant. I didn't even think of that. Maybe you should have my job right now."

"I can wait, old man."

"I'll ignore that. One more thing: there's no way they'll be able to pick all the marijuana seeds out of the soil the flowers are packed in."

"Right, I'll watch for that, too. Since when have you been interested in busting potheads?"

"I'm not. But there's a good chance that there's a connection of some kind with the murders."

"Well, now, that sounds a bit more exciting. Now the only thing I'm wondering is if I should tell Daphne why she's getting flowers every day."

"I'm sure you'll think of something. And if she doesn't want them, give them to me and I'll give them to your mom."

"The hell you will. If I'm going to take the risks, I intend to get the credit."

"Especially since you're not getting paid extra."

"Arnie: I'm a police officer, so anything I discover might come under the Miranda rules. I don't know if you can get a warrant for anything I witness."

"I know. I have some ideas about that; but one step at a time. For right now, we just want to satisfy ourselves that something sketchy is going on there. I could be completely wrong; the coincidences I've observed are actually pretty weak. It's just a gut feeling I have."

Harry finally spoke up. "Your gut feelings are usually pretty good. I think you're on the right track."

"I hope so. If I'm wrong, everything goes back to square one. So, Duane, you in?"

"Hey, you're the boss. But I can't just waltz in there and hang around all day without looking suspicious."

"No, but I think that if you gradually increase the time spent over a few days, Missus Linderman will get to like you enough to enjoy your company for a few hours."

"I guess I could do that; but wouldn't it be easier for Bud and Harry here to just do a stakeout?"

"Like we have time to do that," said Harry.

"I hate stakeouts," said Bud.

"If I'm right about these people, they will be extremely careful and watchful for anybody who might be watching them. Besides, we can't get a warrant just because they see some truck unload some flowers. But you might get a close enough look at these flowers that you could catch a glimpse of a few marijuana leaves mixed in with the flowers. That's evidence 'in plain sight,' and sufficient to support a warrant. I have reason to believe that they've been growing young marijuana plants in the same patches of soil with the flowers. And if they immediately take the flowers into the back room before putting them on the shelves, it suggests that they're going through them and pulling out the pot plants, or at least picking out the marijuana leaves. One more thing: make sure you actually buy some flowers and really give them to Daphne. That way you can legitimately claim to be a customer and that you just happened to notice the evidence in plain sight. Also, you might want to casually admit you're a police officer over in Oak Hill. So, if there's a trial and you have to testify, they can't claim that they were a victim of lying cops without a search warrant. Anyhow, Harry and Bud and I aren't really interested in drugs, so it's very unlikely that you will ever have to testify. Whatever you find out is just meant to give us some direction in our investigation about murder. The only way you would be involved in a murder trial is if you discovered evidence for that in your surveillance, and that is highly unlikely. That being said, if the feds want to use your testimony for securing a warrant for a drug bust, you might have to testify, But like I said, we don't really care about the ATF's case; we just want to find out who killed Tom."

"Should I wear my uniform?"

"I didn't think of that. That might spook them. Tell you what, forget what I said about admitting you're a police officer. I hereby give you a few days off. Better yet, you're fired. You can re-apply for the job in a few days."

"What if you don't hire me again?"

"You forget who I'm living with. Anyway, as of now, you're not a cop. So you have an excuse for not wearing the uniform if it should come up in a trial."

"It just struck me. Will I still get a payheck?"

"Uhhh, no, but I heard your stepfather will make up for it on December twenty fifth."

"Okay, then, this might be fun. Let the speeders and parking violators have a few days flouting the law."

"Good man!"

40

As soon as Duane left the station the next morning to go ingratiate himself with Mrs. Linderman at the flower shop, I went back to thinking about my next move. Nothing immediately came to mind, so I decided to emerge from my stupor and serve the citizens of Oak Hill by doing Duane's job: busting speeders and writing parking tickets. Just as I reached the door. Irma opened it to tell me there was a caller on line 1.

"Chief Crockett."

"Chief, this is Harley from the Fotomat shop in Tulare. I think I've got some information for you."

That perked me up. "Thanks for calling, Mister..."

"Overmeier, Harley Overmeier. Anyway, one of my employees remembers making those copies of that photo you showed me."

"That's good news, go on."

"Well, the customer brought in one of those old photos from the Kodak book, probably the one you showed me, and she made four copies. The next day, they were picked up, along with the original."

"When was this?"

"About a month ago. I can look up the date, if you want."

"I'd appreciate that."

After about three minutes. "Are you still there, chief?"

"Yeah, go ahead."

As I waited, my heart started beating a little faster. A hunch was tugging at it.

"It was September 17, a Friday."

"Did he leave a name?"

"No, and she said he was only a messenger, and didn't know what the copies were for."

"A messenger, really?"

"That's what he said."

"Did he sign for it, or write a check, by any chance?"

"Just a minute, I'll check...he paid with cash."

"Do you know what messenger service he was from?"

"No, but he handed us some kind of cheesy order form."

"'Cheesy?' how?"

"It just looked like it was run off an Apple printer."

"Signed?"

"Yeah."

"Was he the same person who dropped off the original in the first place."

"Yes, he was."

"Uh huh; the same messenger both days." Once again, I admired the meticulous way this killer set up his crime to avoid detection; assuming, of course, the "messenger" was really an uninvolved go-between, which I increasingly doubted.

"Do you still have the form he signed?"

"I do, yes."

"Take good care of it; I'll pick it up as soon as I can. And please be careful handling it. There might possibly be fingerprints. Oh, one more thing. Do you think your clerk would recognize the guy if she ever saw him again?

"Just a minute....she says she thinks so."

The rest of the day, as I collected revenue for the citizens of Oak Hill, I celebrated silently that now I had one more piece of physical evidence. Should I ever arrest a suspect, he could be identified by the photo shop clerk; and the handwriting on the note might link up with somebody whom we can identify - the killer, if we're lucky. Of course, if it was really a messenger and not my perp, I would first have to track him down, which shouldn't be too hard. And if I was REALLY lucky, the form the "messenger" presented might still retain fingerprints, unless he was even cleverer than I thought, and wore gloves. And it occurred to me that he might have even worn some kind of disguise.

When I got back to the office, I called he Fotomat guy again.

"Mister Overmeier, this is Chief Crockett again. Sorry to bother you, but is the clerk who handled the customer who picked up those copies in your shop right now?"

"Yes, she is."

"May I speak to her please?"

"Yes sir? this is Tiffany." The first thing that struck me was that nobody I knew in high school was named Tiffany. It made me feel very old.

"Tiffany, do you recall the man who picked up those copies - what he looked like?"

"Sure. He had a beard and..."

She went on to describe a man who was indistinguishable from the run-of-the mill customer, except for the beard, which she thought was too perfect to be legit, especially since his hair was all messed up. And if he had come in a vehicle, it was not noticed by her. But the thing that sealed the deal for me was that she remembered the customer wearing gloves, which, in the San Joaquin Valley in September, was very much an anomaly. I jotted down the details of what she did recall, including the fact he paid cash; I thanked her, and hung up. Okay, maybe this was my guy. Unfortunately, he left nothing behind, including a usable description, other than being unmistakably male, that might lead me to identify him. Furthermore, he had said very little - deliberately monosyllabic, Tiffany thought. Very careful, it seemed. But I was pretty sure he HAD made his first mistake.

Next, I called Harry and brought him up to date. In return, he informed me that forensics had determined that, as we had suspected, at the murder scenes of Violet and Walter, the glass in the patio door had been cut from the outside and yet, it had been cut from the inside at Tom's murder. A small detail, but a glimpse into the nimble mind of a very punctilious murderer. It was also an indication that there is no such thing as a perfect murder. There are always mistakes made.

In this case, the killer probably never expected forensics detectives to go so far as to microscopically examine the edges of the glass around the holes. But there are murders so carefully planned that only the most thorough investigation can solve them; and this was increasingly shaping up to be just such a crime.

41

After I hung up on Tiffany, I gladly abandoned my plan to collect revenue from unsuspecting passers-through, and headed over to the Fotomat shop in Tulare to pick up that form the "messenger" had left behind, and maybe get anything more that Tiffany might have remembered. On the way, I thought more deeply into just who and where Alicia Bronson might be, assuming she was still alive. She was the nexis of everything, it seemed to me; so I didn't want to leave any stone unturned finding her.

I had already gone through Redwood High School yearbooks looking for Bronson's. I had found three, but only one attended in a year - 1957 - that I thought might have included Alicia, and I remembered that particular student was named Samuel. The natural assumption was that some time before she started high school, Alicia Bronson had moved. I had asked Irma to try to trace a census for Visalia in the '50's, looking for an Alicia Bronson. I already knew she had lived with the now deceased Jewish couple that had adopted Ronald, but I thought perhaps she might have established another residence after leaving Redwood High School.

After picking up the form at the Fotomat and getting no more information, I headed back to visit the other four high schools in Visalia. I was disappointed that I had no better luck finding an Alicia Bronson in any of those schools' records or yearbooks than I had in Redwood's. It appeared that Alicia had not just moved out of her childhood neighborhood, she had moved away from Visalia. Heck, she could be in Tahiti, by now, for all I knew; and if she was, I was screwed.

Unless, of course, she had gotten married and was living in the valley with a different surname.

After departing dejected from Mt. Whitney High School, I headed southwest back toward Tulare. Just to cover all bases, I decided to check out high schools in Tulare. Like Visalia, Tulare had 5 high schools. It was getting late, and I figured I didn't have time to visit them all that day; I'd probably have to come back the next day. The first one I passed coming into town from the east on Highway 127, was Union High School. For once I got lucky - REALLY lucky! In the school's 1960 yearbook, with a sharp, clear graduation photo, was an Alicia Bronson, and there weren't likely any others in the San Joaquin Valley; this was my girl. But that wasn't all; although Alicia's address wasn't available, the high school was only about a mile from the flower shop. Coincidences. Coincidences. Coincidences. I studied that photo carefully but couldn't definitely say, one way or the other after the passage of so many years but it kind of looked a lot like someone I knew whose given name was Alice. I slapped my forehead for not making that name connection earlier.

I really wanted more than anything to drive to the flower shop and confront Mrs. Linderman, but it would have disrupted Duane's ability to collect evidence there on which the ATF could act. So I checked the local phone book, and an Alice Linderman was listed. But there was not another Linderman listed; so she was probably either a widow or divorced. If she was Alicia Bronson, she had apparently moved to her present address sometime after 1960. I bet myself that, when I got back to the station, Irma would have already come to the same conclusion if she managed to access the census records, unless, of course, Miss Bronson became Mrs. Linderman before the census was taken, which was doubtful.

As long as I was in town, I stopped at the Sheriff's Department and left a message for Harry or Bud to contact me as soon as possible. I was hoping they could put surveillance on Mrs. Linderman's home. Who knows? the guy in the "beard" might show up or be living there.

As long as I was in the neighborhood, I decided to once again annoy the people at the Fotomat. Mr. Overmeier introduced me to young Miss Tiffany Schwartz. She was not more than twenty, and I suspected she was eager to get married and acquire a surname more euphoniously appropriate for a Tiffany. I was hoping she would remember a woman having visited the shop - Mrs. Linderman, perhaps? But I had overstepped my luck in Tulare, I guess. It turned out that it was only this one man. She described him as maybe in his mid-20's, good-looking, and pleasant. She couldn't recall any unusual features that would help identify him other than the small, overly-neat beard. She said he claimed to be a messenger from someone else he didn't identify; and there was no business heading on the suspicious order form he gave her. But what had struck her as odd was that he was so particular and anxious about the quality of the copies he was ordering; it seemed out of place for just a messenger. She quickly found the form he signed ordering the copies. The name on the form was, as Mr. Overmeier had said, illegible. Or nearly so. With considerable concentration with a magnifying glass - standard equipment at a photo shop - the name appeared to be "Bill Johnson." That made it hard to run him down, which he probably knew when he signed it. "Bill Johnson" indeed. Besides, the signature looked shaky and heavy, like maybe he had signed it slowly with his non-dominant hand. I carefully dropped the form into a vegetable bag I had brought along. Oak Hill didn't have room in their budget for actual evidence bags. On the way out of Tulare, I stopped again at the Sheriff's station. This time, Harry was working, and I was able to provide him with the signed form from which to try to identify the "messenger." He also said he would try to find someone to keep an eye on the Linderman house.

42

When I got back to the station, Duane had already returned. I stopped at Irma's cubicle and, sure enough, she had found Alicia Bronson listed in the 1960 census records. So I pushed my luck and set her to work on the 1970 and 1980 censuses looking for Alice Linderman and comparing the addresses. If they were the same, that was pretty much proof that Alicia and Alice were the same person, which would have been a huge leap forward in the investigation.

"Are you sure it's 'censuses' and not 'censi,' Arnie?"

"I'll trust your learned judgment, Irma."

As soon as we got settled in my office, Duane reported his progress, such as it was.

"I only stayed for about an hour, so I wouldn't look suspicious the first day. I can make it a little bit longer each day. Missus Linderman was pretty friendly and helpful in helping me pick out a bouquet for Daphne; but I didn't question her about anything. I did keep my eyes open for deliveries and any little signs that there had been any marijuana in the shop. I did see a few seeds that could have been cannabis, but they could just as easily been hemp."

"And would it be likely that there would be hemp in a flower shop?"

"Got me, I'm no flower expert."

"That makes two of us."

"Anyway, I did think that there was a slight odor of marijuana near the rear of the shop, but I couldn't be sure. And there were no deliveries made of any kind while I was there. Likewise, no suspicious people picking up suspicious packages. It looked like nothing more than a flower shop doing flower business. Anyhow, I'll hang around a little longer, tomorrow."

"Good job, Duane."

"Ah, my new daddy, you haven't heard the most interesting part."

"Which is...?"

"Which is the fact that I spent most of my time talking, not to Mrs. Linderman, but to the clerk she said she hired to replace her last one."

"Violet Strand."

"That would be my guess, but I didn't ask."

Good decision. And was there something about her that you found interesting?"

"It wasn't a 'her,' it was a 'him' - Missus Linderman's son, Grover."

"Describe him."

When he finished describing the young Mr. Linderman, I was pretty sure I had found "Bill Johnson," sans beard.

Irma came in, with a big smile on her face.

"Good news, Arnie; a Monte Linderman was listed in the 1970 census, living at the same address as Alicia Bronson in 1960. So, I guess she got married and they decided to live at her house."

"Sounds logical."

"Indeed it is, Mister Spock," intoned Duane, ominously.

"What the hell are you talking about?"

"Didn't you ever watch 'Star Trek' on TV?"

"Nope. Don't like science fiction, because it's a lot of fiction and very little science."

"Well, there's a character on the show that's always going around saying, 'It's only logical.'"

"Take your word for it."

Irma opened my office door.

"Laurel and Hardy are here to see you."

In walked Arthur Granger and Myron Mesmer, each of whom gave Irma a curious look.

"What the hell's she talking..."

"Don't worry about it, Art. She's always joking around. What can I do for ATF's two most intrepid agents?"

"Thanks to you, we feel we're ready to raid that flower farm up in the Sequoias. Judge signed the warrant."

"Good; so what do you want me for?"

"Hey, Arnie, just thought you'd like to get in on the bust, since you set it up."

I was about to say no, because I have no interest in busting pot farmers, but I realized that I might get a chance to find some evidence for my murders up there.

"Thanks, I think I'll take you up on that."

"All right, chief, we'll pick you up right here at three thirty tomorrow morning."

"THREE THIRTY? Now I'm not so sure..."

"Too late, you're coming. You, too, deputy, if Arnie wants."

"Duane's got more important business to do, tomorrow."

"Suit yourself. Dress warm."

43

When I got to the station all bleary-eyed the next morning, Art and Myron were already waiting.

"So how's this going down?"

"Well," said Art, "we're not going up the main road - 180. We're going to take the other route. It's a forest service road, the 13S something."

"13S06," contributed Myron.

"Right. Ever been on it?"

"No, never have. Is it a paved road?"

"No, and it's very narrow and winding all the way up for about ten miles; but as far as we can tell, they don't post any kinds of sentries or lookouts on that route."

Then I suggest we take my old Cherokee instead of that piece of shit you guys drive; it's never gonna make it if there's as much snow as I saw when I went up there."

"I hope you've got a heater - one that doesn't make all that racket your A.C. does."

"I do."

"Fine with us. We'll have another ATF vehicle - four wheel drive; and the Tulare Sheriff's deputies will be joining us with their own SUV's. Plus, we even have a SWAT vehicle full of deputies from the Bakersfield Sheriff's Department. Right before we get to the Lake, we'll park on a street called Yellow Hammer Lane."

"I know it. That's where I parked the other day. It's a good spot. It's a short walk to the compound and lots of trees to hide our approach."

"Well, we'd better get started," said Art, "we should just about be getting there when the sun comes up and these guys are their sleepiest, assuming they do have guards."

"Well, they sure did when I was there, along with mean dogs, electrified fences, and motion-sensing alarms."

"Gee," said Myron, "just for some flowers?"

"Hey, I've been meaning to ask you, Art; if you can tell me who your undercover guy is there?"

"No harm in telling you now. His name is Earl Sturgess."

Omigod! Earl? He's not the guy I met at the barbershop, is he?"

"Could be, it's his favorite place to hang out doing his good ol' boy schtick."

"Well, he sure as hell fooled me."

It was a slow, winding, slushy drive up the service road, and we never encountered any signs of sentries along the way. When we got to Yellow Hammer Lane, we turned left and drove about a hundred yards to a clearing. We bundled up and took our weapons as we left our vehicles and started following the SWAT van up the road. As soon as we reached the front of the compound, lights came on and four men with assault rifles stepped out from the metal shed. Instantly, Art called out over his megaphone.

"This is the FBI and the Bakersfield Sheriff's Department. Put down your arms, NOW! We have a legal warrant to search these premises." Strictly speaking, it wasn't the FBI; it was the ATF, but Art thought FBI sounded more intimidating. Suddenly, one of the guards foolishly raised his weapon with apparent intent to fire towards the officers. The air was suddenly filled with a roar and he was immediately riddled with bullets, and the other three immediately threw down their guns and raised their hands. It actually shocked me; as soon as I saw the rifle raised, I hit the dirt. Art flashed the warrant in the face of one of the other guards, and a pair of deputies checked the corpse, while two others handcuffed the stunned guards and put them in the van, Myron immediately went to the gate and tested for electrification by grounding it with a metal rod of some kind. There was none, so, he removed the lock with a heavy-duty bolt cutter. I went in first, because I knew where the marijuana plants were hidden. A pair of dobermans snarled menacingly, but they were securely restrained on chains. ATF agents brought in plastic tubs and started gathering pots of flowers with marijuana entwined in them. There were so many they filled up all the available vehicles, including mine. They actually had to leave some behind for a later pick-up. Art, Myron, and I went directly to the small office in the shed. It, too, had a padlock which had to be removed. Inside was a safe, which was removed to the SWAT van. A couple of sheriff's deputies were left with the corpse to await a coroner's vehicle.

By the time we got back to the sheriff's office in Visalia, it was ten A.M. After locking up the three surviving guards, we set about to find someone to open the safe. The fourth member of the contingent of security guards, now deceased, was on his way to the morgue in Bakersfield.

With the help of a local blacksmith (yes, they still have those in some towns, like mine), we got the safe open. Inside, there was a little cash and a few documents; but in the main, it was full of ledgers and notebooks. Art, Myron, and I started going through them. Mostly they consisted of what appeared to be financial transactions between the people who ran the flower farm, and those to whom they were selling flowers, et al. There seemed to be two somewhat disparate ledgers. We figured one kept track of legitimate business transactions with flowers only, and the other contained both flower and marijuana sales, though there was no specific mention of marijuana. The term "other flowers" was used in one ledger but not the other, and the amount of money indicated in that ledger was significantly larger than in the other, so we assumed that the "other flowers" were marijuana plants. That excited Laurel and Hardy, but I couldn't have cared less, because there was really nothing here that linked up obviously with the murders. There was no evidence here that indicated which shops were legit and which weren't; everything in both ledgers was officially considered "flowers." However, as I had hoped and expected, The Promises Floral Emporium was one of the customers listed in the ledger with the expensive "other flowers." But what really caught my attention were two names in smaller spiral notebooks separate from where the flower shops were listed: Walter Knobb and Grover Linderman - our first clear link between the son of the owner of the flower shop and one of the killers of the boy on the tricycle. Coincidences... Our assumption was that this notebook contained the names of middlemen between the wholesaler at Hume Lake and the individual outlets, which all appeared to be flower shops. The list did not include Home Depot, Wal-Mart, or other major retailers, as implied by the guys at the barber shop. It was a treasure trove for the ATF. For me, though, it was a mixed blessing, because I was sure the ATF wanted to raid the flower shops as soon as possible. But I was not interested in what was going on vis a vis drug crimes; I just wanted to know who killed Tom and the others. If the ATF raided The Promises Emporium, my investigation could be stalled, because I had no actual evidence yet of murder to hang on any of the principals involved. I needed to have Duane continue to do his undercover thing. So I pleaded with Art and Myron.

"Look, guys, If you'll give Duane and me a little more time, we might get the evidence we need for murder charges."

To my mild surprise, notably absent from any of the notebooks were the names of Alice Linderman or Cory Matcher. I called in Duane from the outer office. He had been hard at work on his computer tracking down the name or names of the owners of the flower farm but hadn't found anything, yet.

"Duane, I want you to try to get to know this Grover Linderman guy a lot better."

"I understand your position, Arnie," said Art, "and I sympathize, but our job is the drug operation, not homicide."

"Hey, look at it this way: Duane will be gathering evidence for BOTH drug deals going on in the shop and trying to spot a murderer. And you guys can still run surveillance on the shop. The more evidence Duane gets, the stronger will be your drug case."

"You do have a point. Okay, look, Arnie, we are going to try to put a lid on the publicity over this morning's bust, but it will be a few days, at most, before the customers discover what happened and they all scatter to the four winds. They probably haven't heard anything about it, yet, because the people we arrested are being held incommunicado and haven't had any chance to warn anyone about the raid.

"Yeah, Art, and you've still got their names and the evidence against them, even if they do start to rabbit."

"Okay, Arnie, we owe you for setting up this bust, so we'll give you a few days, no more."

"Thanks, I really appreciate it."

Now, I really had some serious investigating to do in a hurry.

After Laurel & Hardy left, I cradled my head on my arms on my desk, and started to take a nap, because I was very tired. As I drifted off, I turned everything I had so far over in my mind, trying to make some sense of it all.

44

The central theme of these murders was the one, huge, undeniable factor linking them all: the photo of the boy on the tricycle - Ronald Schlesinger. The other clear fact was that some of the people - victims and perpetrators alike - seem to have been involved in large-scale marijuana trafficking. Which ones? But what bothered me most was what, if anything, had each of these two facts to do with the other? My only real interest was the murder investigation; but could I solve it while ignoring the drug connection? Were the murders mainly prompted by drug deals, and the photos nothing more than a red herring? I doubted that very much. The last thing on my mind before I fell sleep was that it looked like I was going to have to make another visit to the flower shop in Tulare.

A familiar voice roused me from my reverie. "So, Arnie, did you find anything about who might have killed Tom?"

I rubbed my eyes and waited for Irma to come into sharp focus. "Nothing definitive. Walter Knobb, who was one of the kids who killed Ronald Schlesinger was listed in a notebook along with Grover Linderman. They both were apparently buying and selling marijuana."

"Who's Grover Linderman?"

"Oh, didn't I tell you? He's the son of the owner of the flower shop in Tulare, Duane informed me. And it looks like she was the sister and playmate of Ronald when he was killed. The difficulty is that she doesn't look like any killer I ever came in contact with. She just seems like a nice, sweet, middle-aged lady. Grover - her son - on the other hand, doesn't seem incapable of murder, but what would his motive be? He wasn't even born till a good decade after Ronnie was killed. They never knew each other. Maybe he was just doing his mother's bidding."

"Yes, but think about this, Arnie. Which one of them could have gotten into Tom's house without suspicion?"

"You're right. When Duane takes over as chief, you two should make a great crime-fighting duo."

"So, Arnie, you're saying that Duane should be the chief, even though I've been here longer."

"I'm sorry, Irma, you're right. That's pretty sexist of me, isn't it? But as a practical matter, the next chief will have to be elected, and..."

"...not only would it be hard for a woman to get elected, but downright impossible for a Japanese woman, in these parts."

"I'm afraid you're right, Irma. Sorry."

"That's okay. I have no interest in being chief. Besides, I think my parents would have heart attacks if that happened."

"Right. How old are they now?"

"Mom's 63 and dad is a year older."

"Do they still hold a grudge against the government?"

"Would you blame them if they did?"

"No, of course not."

"Well, I suspect they do, but they never talk about it."

45

By the next morning, I had made up my mind which way I wanted to go next. Being possessed of an ability to organize things on paper, I took out some notebook paper and began outlining everything I knew so far, and everything I needed to find out. It went something like this:

A. photo
1) who?
a) Ronald Schlesinger?
a) connection to musketeers
2) Why was it left at the murders?
B. four musketeers
1) Violet Strand
2) Walter Knobb
3) Cory Matcher
4) Gordon Prospero - Phoenix?
C. Alicia Bronson/Schlesinger
1) still alive
2) where?
D. Alice Linderman
1) Alicia?
2) murderess?
E. Grover Linderman
1) "Bill Johnson"?
2) murderer?
F. Cory Matcher
1) murderer?

2) potential victim?
G. Lionel Carmody
1) knew musketeers in school
2) motive for murder?
3) made connection to flower shop/Alicia?
H. hiring of Strand at flower shop coincidence?
I. alternate theory unconnected to Linderman
1) musketeers into drug dealing? Cartel?
2) Matcher eliminating competition?
a) why photo?
b) solid alibi

Then I went back and crossed out the items that made Cory Matcher a suspect. He didn't do it.

As I stared at the as yet incomplete outline, Irma popped her head inside my office.

"Arnie. Line 2."

I punched the #2 button. "Chief Crockett."

"Arnie. It's Harry. I just wanted to bring you up to date on our end of the investigation. Yesterday, Bud and I decided to track the phone records of both Walter Knobb and Violet Strand."

"And?"

"And they had phone contact prior to the murders."

"Really?"

"Yeah, Knobb called her twice and she called him once only about two weeks before Knobb was killed."

"Interesting." I jotted that down as the next item on my outline:

"J. Strand/Knobb connection?"

"But that's not all. Both of them had phone contact with the Promises Emporium Flower Shop. Which is to say, that someone from the flower shop called Strand, but only once."

"That's also very interesting. Knobb was almost certainly mixed up in the marijuana operation; you don't think Strand was, also, do you?"

"I can't imagine that," said Harry.

"Nor can I. But I guess we can't rule it out. But the fact that two of the four 'musketeers' were in contact before both were murdered takes coincidence to a whole new level. If you haven't already done it, I suggest you check Cory Matcher's phone records, as well. And I'll call Phoenix and have them check Gordon Prospero's. If he was in contact with the others, that pretty much nails down the 'four musketeers' connection as the motive, since it is unlikely they were in the marijuana selling business together at that distance."

"Okay, Arnie, will do; anything for us?"

"Well, I guess you know about the big ATF bust of the flower farm in Hume, yesterday?"

"Yeah, did you find out anything there?"

I filled them in and informed them that the three surviving security guards were being transferred to federal lock-up in Bakersfield.

"Okay, Arnie, we'll let you get back to your Sherlocking, and we'll do our flatfoot thing. Check with you later."

As I was hanging up, Duane came into the office.

"Just letting you know, Arnie: I'm off to buy some flowers again."

"Right. Look, Duane, you might not be on this as long as I planned, since the ATF will probably raid the place in a couple of days. I'd just as soon you weren't there when it happens, 'cuz they'd have to arrest you and haul you in, just to protect your identity."

"Maybe I shouldn't go at all, since they seem to have all the evidence they need from the raid."

"Well, there won't be any wholesale deliveries to watch for, now. But it's still possible that some street dealers might come in to buy their supply and you can try to spot their license plates, if they come in cars. The more evidence we can give the ATF the better, if only to keep us on their good side. But what I really want you there for is to get to know the Linderman's well enough that they might let down their defenses and let something slip about the murders. So, let's shoot for two more days. You don't need to spend as long as you have been, though; they might be less suspicious if you don't hang around too long."

"Got it."

"And one more thing: If I should happen to show up at the shop while you're there, act surprised. Show that you recognize the Chief Constable of Oak Hill."

"Why?"

"If this thing goes to court, we don't want to be accused of some kind of set up - that you pretended not to know me."

"Got it."

I had all but decided that it was time for confronting the "persons of interest" directly. Based on my outline, the only possible suspects would be linked to the flower shop. In fact, I had already begun planning a little surprise for one of them; but which one I wasn't quite sure, yet. I spent the rest of the day expanding, refining, and studying my outline. I also called detectives in Phoenix to ask about their phone records check on Prospero. It turned out they'd already finished it, and that there were no phone contacts between Prospero and anybody in the San Joaquin Valley. That tended to further eliminate drug dealing as a motive. There were no two ways about it: everything intersected at the flower shop in Tulare. So I spent the last couple of hours of the day carefully formulating my approach in questioning the Linderman's the following day. It would be a delicate balancing act: letting them know they were in jeopardy without actually accusing them. The evidence, so far, though intriguing, was entirely circumstantial. My strategy was to get them to be careless and desperate enough that they would slip up and implicate themselves. Whether that was "they", "he", or "she", I wasn't sure,

46

The next morning, I decided to leave for Tulare before Duane, so he would be prepared for my already being in the shop when he arrived.

When I jingled my way into the shop, I immediately spotted Mrs. Linderman behind the cash register, but otherwise, the place seemed deserted.

Mrs. Linderman's son did not seem to be around as I started out with idle pleasantries to allay any nervousness she might have had about my surprise visit.

"Good morning, Missus Linderman, how are you this morning?"

"Fair to middlin'. How about yourself?"

"Well, I woke up this morning. That's a point in my favor."

"Better than the alternative."

"Ha ha, ain't it the truth."

As we chatted, Mrs. Linderman was very cordial with what seemed to be genuine friendliness and no hint of shock or surprise. If she was a murderess, she was a darned cool one. But then, I already knew that whoever it was had to be a cool customer.

"So, Chief Crockett. I'm happy to see you again, but have you learned any more about poor Violet's murder?" I was glad she brought up the subject and not I.

"A few things, yes. But I wanted to clear up a few minor points that you might be able to help me with, if you would."

"I'm happy to do whatever I can."

I pulled out the photo. "Remember when I showed you this?"

No visible reaction. "I do, yes, but I have no idea who that boy is."

"Was."

"What?" This time her eyelid flicking rate picked up a little and she didn't look up at me.

"This boy was murdered back about the time you were his age."

She kept staring at the photo, until tears started coming.

"Oh my god. Is this a picture of Ronnie?"

"We don't know for sure. I was hoping you could tell me. You were Alicia Bronson..."

For the first time, she reacted with a surprised expression, but immediately got control of herself. "Yes. Ronnie was my brother. Not my real brother; he was adopted."

"Yes, I knew that."

She did her best to hide her surprise, but her mind must have been going a mile a minute.

"So now you think this is a photo of Ronald?"

"Could be. What do you think?"

"Well, this boy looks like he's about four. I was a year younger, so I can't really be sure."

"I understand that. Missus Linderman, were you aware of the fact that Violet Strand was one of the teenagers who is believed to have been responsible for Ronald's death? You didn't happen to know that, did you?"

"No, of course not. I'd have never hired her if I'd known."

"Missus Linderman, were you a witness to Ronald's killing?"

"ME? Absolutely not. Why do you ask that?"

"I was hoping that, since you two were about the same age, with no other siblings, you might have hung out together a lot and might have been together when the four musketeers sent him plunging down that hill on his bike."

First slip-up. She showed no surprise when I told her how the "Four Musketeers" had done it. Because she already knew. But she recovered quickly.

"No, I was at home when the police came and told us about it."

"I notice that you didn't ask me who the "four musketeers were."

She hesitated, then, "The four who?" Now she was noticeably nervous.

"That's what the kids who a couple of people I've talked to have told me were responsible for Ronald's death called themselves. According to the records I've been able to turn up, none of the kids was charged with any crime, so maybe Ronnie decided on his own to try to ride down 'Devil's Slide.'"

My comment hit its intended target. She thought about it for a moment and said, meekly, "He would never have done that. He was only just learning to ride a bike." And she started crying out loud with copious tears. I waited her out before continuing. One thing was clear: for this woman, the half century or so or so since her brother was killed had not lessened her pain.

When she stopped, I hit her again. "Like I said, I noticed you didn't ask me who the 'four musketeers' were." The cops didn't know about that, so they never told you.".

"I seem to remember somebody mentioning them when I was a kid. You think they killed Ronnie?" Fast thinking.

"Very likely. Well, here's the thing, Missus Linderman. Somebody left copies of this picture at three of the killings - all except Chief Whiting's."

"What about..." She stopped cold and froze.

"What about what?" I kept my fingers crossed that she would say "What about Lionel Carmody?" But no such luck.

"Nothing, just wondering." But she had already spoken volumes, as far as I was concerned.

"The first one, left by Mister Knobb's body, didn't raise any suspicions - just a photo of a kid on his nightstand. They did fingerprint it, but found no prints at all. That was the killer's first mistake, because the only logical explanation for no fingerprints being found on a photo that must have been frequently handled is that they were wiped off. But the real clincher - the BIG mistake - was leaving an identical picture at the other murders. Apparently, the killer thought no cops would notice. And we didn't, for awhile. But once we did, there was absolutely no doubt that the kid was connected in some way to the murder; so I busted my butt for days finding out who he was. And that's why I'll eventually catch him. My investigation points very strongly to this being a picture of Ronald Schlesinger. And if it is, it gives us motive. Whoever killed these people is extremely intelligent and clever. He masterfully covered all his tracks. But he made that one huge blunder. In fact, if he hadn't, I doubt that we would ever have been able to catch him." She clearly took comfort at my use of the masculine pronoun.

"But why do you think he left those photos?"

"Obsession. He held such a deep hatred for these people that he wanted to send them to hell with a reminder of why. And he hoped no one else, like us dumb cops, would realize it."

Just then, in walked Duane, who acted surprised to see me.

"Hey, chief. What're you doin' here?"

"Just checking in with Missus Linderman; how about you?"

"Hey, I wanted to buy Daphne some flowers for Christmas."

"Daphne? Oh, you mean your girl friend?"

"Right."

"And flowers is all you're going to get her for Christmas?"

"Of course not, but every little bit helps."

As far as I could tell, our little charade was not arousing any suspicions in Mrs. Linderman. He turned toward her.

"Hi, Missus Linderman; I want to get some more flowers for my fiancé"

Mrs. Linderman wiped her eyes and smiled weakly. "Of course, young man. Look around, I'll be with you when I'm finished with Chief Crockett."

"Sure. I guess Grover's not around?"

She looked down at her tightly-clasped hands as she quietly said, "No, not this morning."

I interrupted. "Well, I'll be getting out of your hair. I just wanted to let you know how the investigation into your friend's death is going."

"My friend? He was my...oh, you mean Violet. Thank you, chief. I wish you luck."

"Thanks, I could use some luck. But I think I have a very good lead to follow. I may know by tomorrow who it was who had the copies of this photo made. I'm going to all the photo shops from here to Visalia, even Bakersfield if I have to, until I find out who it was; because, whoever it was is very much involved in these murders." She didn't say anything, but struggled to maintain a pleasant smile as I left. I deliberately did not inform her that I'd already found the photo shop in question and that I suspected that the customer in question - "Bill Johnson" - was, in reality, her son, Grover.

"Before you leave, chief, could I offer you a bouquet to give your wife for the holidays - no charge?"

"Thanks anyway, ma'am, that's nice of you, but I'm not married; I'm divorced with no kids, so I live alone." Out of the corner of my eye, I caught Duane suddenly swiveling his siidelong gaze towards me, since I had just discounted the existence of his mother, sister, and dog.

"Oh, that's a shame, not even any pets for company?"

"No ma'am, I'm strictly a loner, and I like it that way." I don't lie often, but when I do, I think I'm pretty good at it, especially when I have a good reason, which was the case, here.

As I left, I wondered why Grover wasn't at work, this morning. I hoped he wasn't out stalking Cory Matcher. Just to be sure, on the way back to the station, I stopped at the Jiffy-Lube where he worked and warned him to watch his back, because I was almost certain he was the next target for the killer since he is the only "musketeer" left. Or should I say "D'artagnan"? That scared the daylights out of him, which is exactly what I wanted to do; he had once helped kill a little kid and had gotten away with it. The least I could do was make his life as miserable as possible. What I didn't tell him was that I suspected the actual next target for the killer would not be him, but me, for the same reason my friend, Tom, was killed. But he had not been expecting it. I was.

47

Back at the station, I resumed studying my outline. I read it over and over, and with each reading I solidified one inescapable conclusion: I had absolutely no evidence to arrest anyone. I decided that there was only one possible way I could catch the killer, and I had just initiated the first step in the process. I also had decided who the killer had to be. Trouble is, I had zero evidence that would ever bring a search warrant, much less an indictment. Every bit of the evidence I had was weakly circumstantial, based almost entirely on my tenuous, personal conclusions about coincidences - legally useless. Nevertheless, it was sufficient to make my jigsaw puzzle all but complete in my mind. Duane came in.

"So, Duane, anything interesting, today?"

"Well, not much, except that, just as soon as you left, Missus Linderman got on the phone and had a hushed conversation that she clearly didn't want overheard."

"I don't suppose you know who it was?"

"No, but I can make a pretty good guess, because about half an hour later her son came in and they hurriedly went in the back room. I could see them talking excitedly, but I couldn't hear what they were saying."

"I think I know what they were talking about."

"And would that have something to do with that lie you told Missus Linderman about living alone?"

"It would."

"So, what can I do to help?"

"You can take your mom and Nancy to your house and put

them up for a day or two - three at the most. If something's going to happen, it will happen fast."

"I think I see what you have in mind, but can't I help? If you're going to do what I think you're going to do, shouldn't you have back-up?"

"I don't think so; besides, if you're helping me, who's protecting your mom and Nancy?"

"What about Harry and Bud?"

"First of all, I'm going by a gut feeling here. If I get them all involved and I turn out to be wrong, which is entirely possible, I'll look like a fool and so will they."

"But you'll be alive."

"Believe me, I'll be careful."

"How're you going to explain it to mom?"

"I guess I'll tell her the truth; she'll understand. Of course, Nancy Drew may want to get in on it, so she'll be disappointed that she can't. Actually, I won't tell her anything."

"Okay, Arnie, bring them over tonight and we'll try to make it a pre-Christmas sleepover party, or something."

"Thanks, Duane, that's a load off my mind."

"Sure. Getting back to the flower shop. There was one more thing of interest that happened today. While I was picking out flowers for Daph, a young man came in who went to the counter and quietly asked for his flower delivery, but he kept looking around kind of hinky, especially at me. Without a word, Grover went into the back and came out with a cardboard box that was taped shut. The customer turned it over and gave Grover a stack of cash that looked like an awful lot for a box of flowers, if you get my drift."

"I do, indeed. The Linderman's evidently don't know about the Hume Lake raid."

"So, as he was leaving, I sort of edged over to the window display and managed to catch his license plate number as he drove away in a beat-up old white Dodge pick-up. I noticed he didn't put the box in the bed of the truck, but in the seat next to him. Clearly, it was a valuable package."

"Good job, Duane; I'll let Laurel and Hardy know right away."

"One more thing. I did try to engage Grover in a casual conversation, but he was clearly more concerned about what his mother had just told him than in anything I had to say."

48

That night, Duane came over for a dinner of mashed potatoes, gravy, steamed vegetables, franks, beans, and corned beef hash. I saved my announcement until we all had our fill.

"Well, you guys, I wanted to let you know that you're all going to have a fun party at Duane's house for a couple of days."

"What in the world are you talking about, Arnie?"

"You and Nancy are going to be guests of your son, here, for a couple of days."

"And why would we be doing that?"

"Sort of a pre-Christmas party."

"What in the world are you talking about; where did you come up with an idea like that?"

"Well, I just wanted to get the house ready for Santa Claus."

"What's a sandaclaws?" asked Nancy. We all stared at her dumbfounded, but the expression on her face never changed.

"You know, Nancy," said Duane, "The jolly fat man in the red suit who brings presents on Christmas Eve."

"Presents? Really?"

It suddenly struck me that Nancy had lived all her life in that remote encampment below Wolfskill Peak, and Christmas was just one of the things about civilization that the psycho killer, Esau Reinart, never allowed amongst his flock of followers. Duane, apparently not noticing that his new sister was eleven years old, now, decided to tell her about Santa Claus. When he finished, Nancy just giggled over such an absurd notion, which, frankly, made me even more proud of her.

"Oh, Duane, you're so silly. Who ever heard of flying all around the world with a bunch of flying deer and climbing down all the fireplaces in the world with a sack full of presents? Who'd ever be stupid enough to believe something like that?"

Marjorie is no fool. She sensed that she and Nancy were being removed from the house because I was worried that they might be in danger. But, bless her heart, she said nothing, not wanting to alarm Nancy, though I suspect that if she knew, Nancy would have been the first to demand to stay and face the danger. After she went to her room to pack her doll and Nancy Drew mystery, I told Marjorie everything.

After my family was packed for a short vacation and had driven away with Duane, I got busy. Principally, I had to rig up something that would appear in the dark to be a person, presumably me, asleep in my bed. And, of course, pillows are the ideal means of doing that. When I finished, I stood there looking at the bulges beneath my blankets. They really didn't look like a person sleeping to me, but someone looking at them in the dark and expecting a person would almost certainly see a person, not a pile of pillows. I also rigged up a strong floodlight above my headboard and strung extension cords to my closet, where I plugged it into a multi-jack strip with an on-off switch. Then I settled down inside the closet with the switch on my left side and my .38 on my right. I used one of the remaining pillows to put behind me as I sat back against the wall of the closet. I left the sliding doors cracked open just enough to have a view of my bed.

As I waited, my thoughts focused on why I was forced to do this. There simply wasn't any evidence to charge anyone with these murders. There wasn't any evidence to find, because it simply did not exist. Nor was it likely that any physical or forensic evidence ever would be found. If an arrest was made and there were a trial, any jury member would be justified in acquitting on the basis of reasonable doubt. I would have. I was 90% certain who the killer was, but I simply had nothing to prove it, or even strongly imply it. My belief was based purely on two things: gut instinct, and the fact that nobody else made any sense, given the circumstantial evidence

I had. I had decided that the only piece of real evidence that existed was in the hands of the killer and would be provided to me by him or her. So I waited, and waited, and waited - kind of like when I was at the Porterville airport. I kept shifting around in the dark because my lumbar vertebrae were increasingly aching due to my arthritic scoliosis, which I acquired from having rickets in infancy. Occasionally, I would lean over and lie on the floor of my closet on my side in a fetal position, though I never removed my focus from the crack in the door.

My biggest concern was that my putative stalker would not show up tonight, and I would have to do it all over again the next, and maybe not even then would it happen. But I felt that, if I was right, I had given the killer no other choice. If they killed my friend Tom Whiting, the County Sheriff, they surely wouldn't hesitate to do the same to the chief of a little hick town like Oak Hill. Then, at around 3:00 A.M...

49

I heard it before I saw it. A slight disturbance in the air, a subtle change in the sound of the moving air, and the faint squeak of the hinges on my bedroom door. I quickly got onto one knee and peered though the crack. I picked up my .38. An apparition, dark and hooded, appeared at the foot of my bed and moved slowly up to the head. After a seemingly interminable 30 seconds or so, A gun exploded in a loud crack. I hit the switch, throwing a flood of light onto my apparition, now silhouetted in blinding light. The gun was fired twice more in panic at the wall below the light as I sprang from my nest. Switching the .38 to my left hand, I quickly closed the gap between my closet and my putative killer; I grabbed the pistol and wrenched it from my would-be assassin's hand. At that instant, another loud crack accompanied a sharp pain in my left hip. I fell to the floor and rolled to my right to see a man standing in my bedroom door, clearly lighted by my floodlight. Just as he took a second shot that zipped just over my head, I shot him. I hit him in the middle of the chest and he dropped instantly where he had stood. My pillow assassin screamed.

"Grover! Grover! You've killed my son."

I was pretty sure that I had indeed killed Grover Linderman. For a few seconds I was shocked that, after spending all of my adult years, either in the military or on a police force, this was the first time I had ever shot anyone to death, as far as I knew. I went over to Grover's crumpled body and kicked away his .32 revolver and checked for vital signs, but there weren't any.

Recovering from her initial, paralyzing shock, Alice Linderman, nee Alicia Bronson, rushed to her son's side and cradled him in her ams as she wept uncontrollably. I kept quiet and picked up Grover's handgun with my handkerchief and dropped it into the pocket of my windbreaker. Once she calmed down and got control of herself, I helped her stand and told her she was under arrest for attempted murder as I took the handcuffs I had put in my other jacket pocket out and put them on the anguished woman.

"Murder?" she said, "you have no proof I murdered anyone. You killed my innocent son for no reason."

"You're right, Missus Linderman, I didn't have any evidence whatsoever, so I have you to thank for bringing it with you."

"What do you mean?"

"The gun, Missus Linderman, the gun. This is a .22 revolver I'm holding, and you brought it along. Now I have it and we both know forensics will prove that it killed at least three and maybe four people. Now, would you like to sit on the bed and tell me all about why you did all that killing?"

"The bed? Who did I shoot?"

"You shot some of my pillows, but don't worry, I won't charge you for them. I repeat, do you want to give me your story?"

"I want a lawyer."

"Okay then, we'll say no more about it till the cops and detectives and medical people get here. Then we're going to the police station and you can call a lawyer from there. Just to make it official, I am also placing you under arrest for the murder of Walter Knobb, Violet Strand, Lionel Carmody, and Tom Whiting." My voice choked a bit with the reading of that last name. Mrs. Linderman gave me a curious look that seemed odd, at first.

"Oh, I see, you're wondering why I didn't include Gordon Prospero on that list. You probably won't be charged with that crime, except as a conspiracy, because I don't think you did it, That one wasn't committed with a .22, but a .32, which I'm guessing is the one that's now in my pocket. The slug is now somewhere in this room and the forensics people will find it and link it to Prospero's murder. Anyway, you have the right to remain silent; anything you say can and will be held against you in a court of law. You are entitled to an attorney and to have one present before answering any questions. If you cannot afford an attorney, one will be provided to you, free of charge, before any questioning. Do you understand these rights as I stated them?"

She was thinking about it. "Missus Linderman?"

"I understand."

"Having these rights in mind, do you wish to talk to me without an attorney present?" She answered with her silence.

Everything had gone as planned, except for two things: I hadn't expected Grover to show up, though maybe I should have. And I hadn't expected to be shot. Fortunately the slug was a through and through in the fleshy part of my left buttock, and though it hurt like hell, it would heal.

50

Back at the Oak Hill station, I sat Mrs. Linderman in a chair across from me at my desk. My office doesn't have an interrogation room, but it was much closer to the arrest site than the Tulare office. Harry and Bud were on route. Then they could put her in their interrogation room after i finished with her. I sat with my handkerchief placed over my wound, and I sat on it solidly to keep pressure on it till the blood stopped oozing. I first called Duane and told him the outline of what had occurred and had him tell Marjorie and Nancy that it would be at least another day before they could return home, as detectives and criminalists processed our bedroom as a crime scene. I told Duane to come to the station right away, and I notified Harry and Bud. They were eagerly headed my way. I did not tell any of them I'd been shot.

"You have a family?"

"Yes, Missus Linderman, I have a wonderful family."

"But you said..."

"I lied. Okay, Missus Linderman, here's how it's going to be. You have asked for an attorney, so I don't want to hear anything from you until he gets here; so, do you want to call him, now?"

"He's in bed, besides I don't know his number."

"His name, then?"

"I don't have an attorney."

"Do you want to find one in the yellow pages right now? Or would you rather have a public defender?"

"I don't really care."

"Okay, while we're waiting for the other detectives to get here, I want you to listen very carefully to what I have to say; believe me, it's to your advantage to pay close attention." She said nothing except,

"You murdered my son."

"Believe me, I'm very sorry that became necessary. But here's how things stand. That .22 you shot into my pillows will certainly match up with the other murders and prove beyond any reasonable doubt any jury might consider to prove that you did indeed murder those people. By this time tomorrow, I'm sure that either the tires on your car or Grover's will match the tire prints left at Mister Carmody's murder. Furthermore, one of those victims was a sheriff beloved by everybody in Tulare County, so it is very likely that the state will seek the death penalty against you, now that it has been reinstated in California. At this point, I'm pretty much out of the picture, so I don't really care whether or not they decide to execute you, though I'd prefer they didn't. I'm not driven by vengeance the way you are. However, I am very interested in what drove you to do all this killing. It is quite possible that your story of feeling the need for revenge for a terrible injustice done to you as a child will sway a jury to be lenient in sentencing you. Furthermore, your lawyer may very well try to defend you on an insanity plea in order to save you life."

"I'm not insane."

"Maybe not, but when a jury hears the story of a woman who carried a desire for revenge around for more than forty years for something that happened to you when you were six, they just might be persuaded that you don't really have all your marbles. They might even send you away to a looney bin, which is okay with me, as long as you spend the rest of your days there.

"Why do you care?"

"To tell you the truth, I don't care all that much, except that you killed one of my closest friends, who had no roll in what happened to Ronald; otherwise, I might have had more sympathy for you. But I'm trying to convince you that, by telling your whole story it may save your life; and it's your story I want to hear. I think I already know the main facts, but there's much that still puzzles me, and I want to convince you that, by helping me understand, you may help yourself as well.

"I'll think about it."

51

Early the next morning, Alice Linderman, AKA Alicia Bronson, was transferred to the jail at the Tulare County Sheriff's Station, as Grover was taken to the morgue. Before she was arraigned for first degree murder with special circumstances (multiple murders), which meant she was eligible for the death penalty, she was brought into an interrogation room, where Harry and I, in the presence of the public defender, Orville Masters, began questioning her and recording her statements.

For the most part, she remained silent and stoically refused to answer our questions. Harry and I again reminded her, as well as her attorney, that the gun she used to try to kill me was absolutely the gun that killed all her victims, and Mr. Masters began whispering in her ear, probably advising her that her best chance at avoiding the death penalty would be to tell us her whole story, in hopes that it would create some empathy on the part of jurors, especially those who were less than enthusiastic about the death penalty. Actually, neither was I. He did not, however, mention the insanity plea option, though, based on the nature of his interruptions, he was clearly considering it. Harry pointed out that the district attorney might even be willing to offer a plea bargain of a life sentence if she would plead guilty and tell her whole story, which everybody wanted to hear.

After about two hours, Mrs. Linderman finally said,

"Oh what the hell. I did it. I killed them all, and I'm not sorry. My life is over anyway, so I don't give a damn what they do to me. I'll confess to killing Gordon, too."

Harry and Bud let me do the rest of the interrogation. "We both know," I said, "that you didn't kill Mister Prospero, your son did, and I'm sorry, but he's beyond saving, now."

"My only regret is that I didn't get Cory Matcher. I think I hated him more than any of them."

"If it makes you feel any better, Mister Matcher has not only admitted to what he did, he convinced me that he is genuinely remorseful, and believes it was a horrible thing he did that haunts him to this day."

"Good, but he deserved to die, too."

"So, are you willing to tell us everything, from the beginning? It will probably be your last chance."

"Sure, why not? I'm proud of what I did; it was something that had to be done, and I did it." With that, she launched into her extraordinary story.

52

"My father and mother were able to escape from Hungary in 1934 when Hitler was trying to kill all the Jews he could. Thanks to the wonderful Swedish hero, Raoul Wallenberg, they were able to be smuggled out of the country and, after several years in England, I was born in 1943, and they were eventually able to come to America. I don't remember any of this, of course, because I was only an infant. The synagogue in Visalia took us in and cared for us. Eventually, my father made a good living as a real estate broker. One of the families who were members of the congregation, the Schlesinger's, rented an apartment two doors down from ours. Not long after I was born the Schlesinger's were killed in an auto accident and the synagogue arranged for my parents to adopt Ronnie, who had survived the accident. They saw it as doing their godly duty. Ronnie was only about a year older than me, and we got to be playmates and loved each other like a real brother and sister. But it wasn't just that he was my playmate. He was my protector, my teacher, my guide in life. To me, Ronald was the closest thing to god. I followed him everywhere and loved him like no one else in my entire life, before or since.

"Ronnie got a bicycle for Christmas in 1949. He didn't really know how to ride it. He had only previously had a tricycle, and he was very proud of it, as you can see in that picture. But our parents did not attempt to teach him to ride it, and being only seven, it was not easy for him to teach himself. Still, he took it with him wherever he went, trying to find somebody to help him learn, since I didn't know how, either.

"Ronnie was just starting to get the hang of riding the bike when he decided he wanted to go to Devil's Slide to watch the older kids ride their bikes, and maybe get someone to help him learn to ride better. Devil's Slide was about a mile east of where we lived and we walked there with sack lunches to have a picnic. We sat down under a tree and munched on sandwiches while we watched the other kids, about two hundred yards away, playing with their bikes and disappearing over the edge of the steep hill, and we could hear their wild screams shooting down the hill. At first, nobody saw us where we were sitting in the shade of a big willow tree. Then some kid noticed Ronnie's bike and waved at him to come over. That got him all excited and he said he wanted to go take a closer look. He told me to stay where I was, though, because it would be safer. I always did exactly whatever Ronnnie said.

He walked his bike over to the crowd and watched a few kids ride down the hill, but he could see it was scary and started to come back to where I was. But one of the older kids grabbed his bike. I couldn't hear what they were saying, except that Ronnie kept saying that he didn't want to. Then a couple of the bigger boys, including Cory, grabbed him, as another boy and a girl - Violet - held his bike. They forced him onto it, and as he was screaming and crying they wheeled him over to the top of the hill and pushed him over the edge. I could hear him screaming and I hid behind the tree, but I was too scared to run over to help him. For the rest of my life I will always feel terribly ashamed about my cowardice that day. Suddenly all the kids started running and riding their bikes to get away from that place. When they had all left, I ran over to the edge and I could see Ronald and his bike all crumpled up about halfway down the hill. When I reached him, I was in a panic and out of my mind with grief and fear. I called out his name several times, but he didn't answer or even move. I ran home to tell my parents. They ran to the hill and tried to do something to help Ronald, but even I could see that he couldn't be helped. He was dead, covered with blood, and several bones were broken badly.

When we got home my parents called the police who came with an ambulance and took him away. It's the last time I ever saw him.

The police asked me all kinds of questions, but all I could do was cry uncontrollably. I kept telling them and my parents that it was my fault. They were kind and dismissed my guilt, saying it was God's will. I really didn't understand at the time what God had to do with it, and I still don't. I still suffer from the feeling that I might have helped had I not been such a coward.

As I grew up, I could never put what happened out of my mind. But I did come to believe that the main fault was not mine but those kids who pushed him down the hill. So I did everything I could to find out just who they were. It wasn't till I got to high school that I finally identified all four of them, and my friends who had been there told me Cory Matcher, who was the biggest kid and Gordon Prospero were the ones who forced Ronnie onto the bike and held him there, while Walter Knobb and Violet Strand took the handlebars and guided the bike.

Over the years, I guess I just kept fantasizing about killing Ronnie's murderers until I became totally obsessed. But I never planned on actually doing anything about it until the day Walter walked into my flower shop. I recognized his name instantly when my son introduced him. He was a friend of my son's, even though he was much older, and the two of them hung out together getting into trouble. When my son introduced me to Walter, I knew immediately who he was. And here he was, trying to talk me into using my flower shop to sell marijuana he picked up from that place over at Hume Lake. I didn't want to do it, but I thought it was the best way to keep contact with him until I could figure out what to do. Then he happened to mention that an old classmate, Violet Strand, was living over in Visalia. She was yet another of Ronnie's killers. That's when I started to make a plan. Walter and Violet weren't close friends, but they had some contact and I casually mentioned that I would like to find an older woman to help me in the shop. Walter suggested Violet. She was actually a pretty good employee, but I was only interested in finding out all I could about her and fantasizing about killing her. But my more immediate concern was my son's association with Walter.

So I decided to kill him first. My son told me he lived alone, and I started making my plan."

"What gave you the idea of cutting a hole in the glass?"

"Well, first of all, it seemed like the easiest way to get in. I had no idea how to pick locks or anything. And I'm a little too old to be able to climb up to the second floor balcony outside his bedroom."

"How did you know..."

"Grover told me. And I saw on some TV show or movie that showed you could take a diamond and scratch a circular line in glass and punch it out. I even tried it out on an old car window my son had in the garage. But it didn't work. It just shattered into a million pieces. Grover told me that's how automobile windows are made."

"It's called 'safety glass."

"Right. Grover told me that. So I tried it on my bedroom window and I punched it out - clean as a whistle."

"Really? Is it still there?"

"Uh huh. But it's covered up with Saran Wrap" When I went to Walter's house about three in the morning. I put the suction cup near the door handle and kept going around and around holding the diamond tight between my fingers until it made a deep cut. I was wearing my garden gloves and hit the middle of the circle with the heel of my hand. It popped right out, but made hardly any noise at all because it fell onto a mat kept inside to wipe your feet. I snuck upstairs, and went right to Walter's bed where he was sound asleep. Even before I shot him I set the picture of Ronnie next to his head."

"Did you use a silencer?"

"No. I wouldn't have any way of knowing where I could get one. I just put the gun as close to his head as I could without touching him, and that tended to muffle the sound a little. Also, his window was closed."

"I guess a single .22 wouldn't likely wake anybody up who was sleeping soundly, especially since the nearest house was almost a hundred feet away."

"That's what I was counting on.

"How come you left the glass circles at the other murders but took the one from Tom's house with you?"

"I cut myself on it, and didn't want to take time to wash off the blood. So I just dropped it in my pocket."

"But what you didn't count on was that forensics could still determine microscopically on which side of the door the glass was cut. And when they said that the glass at Chief Whiting's house was cut from the inside and the others from the outside, it helped me get a clearer picture of the motive for his murder was compared to the others. Correct me if I'm wrong, but you just knocked at his door and he let you in, right?"

"Yes. When he questioned me I could see that he didn't suspect me yet, but that he was getting closer. So..."

"So you went to his house and put on your sweet old lady act, and when his back was turned..."

"I shot him. Then I went over and cut a circle out of his patio window to make it look like somebody he didn't know, like a burglar or something, came from outside. I even tried to bring the glass circle indoors from outside, but it had broken, and when I tried to pick up the pieces it cut me, so I decided not to leave it."

"What you didn't count on was forensics determining it had been cut from the inside. And you took the circle with you to fool detectives?"

"That, and to have a kind of reminder or trophy of what I was proud of doing."

"You were proud of killing the sheriff?"

"welll..."

"Do you have the pieces hidden at home?"

"Sure, but I'll let your detectives find them without my help."

"Didn't you think you were taking a chance leaving those photos of Ronald at the other killings?"

"Not really. I didn't think it would mean a thing to detectives. And I HAD to make sure Violet and Walter knew why they were going to Hell."

"And you wiped off your fingerprints."

"Yes."

"Big mistake. Assuming detectives might have had a reason for taking your prints, which is doubtful, it wouldn't have been enough evidence to even suspect you, much less arrest you. And I'm pretty sure your prints aren't in any criminal databases. But wiping off those prints told us that they were likely wiped off by the killer. If the victims had put those photos there, they almost surely would have left fingerprints. And when you left a photo at Violet's murder scene, as well..."

"I just didn't think anyone would notice."

"We almost didn't. But cops aren't as dumb as a lotta people think. I can almost guarantee you that you would never have been caught if you hadn't let your hate get the best of you and made you make that mistake. I'm not sure I get why you killed Lionel Carmody. He had nothing to do with Ronald's death."

"He came in my shop one day and asked if I remembered him. I didn't. But he said he was reading in the papers about how Violet and Walter were murdered, and wasn't that a coincidence that we all went to school together at the same time. It turned out that he was friends with them and Cory in high school, and they told him about how they had gotten crazy and accidentally killed Ronnie Schlesinger back when they were in junior high. I guess they told him I was their sister and that I had been asking questions about them. A couple of years later, he read in the paper about my wedding and noticed my maiden name and my married name. Then, right about the time the murders were reported in the paper, he remembered seeing an ad in the paper about the flower shop with me listed as proprietor."

"I saw the same ad. He had it kind of hidden in his house. Did he try to blackmail you?"

"Not directly, no. But he hinted around that he was thinking about going to the police with what he knew and said he'd be back to talk to me about it later. I took that to mean he might have blackmail in mind, or actually go to the police. I decided I couldn't take a chance on that happening."

"I was wondering about your killing of Walter Knobb. Why did you pick that particular night to kill him?"

"He happened to tell me over the phone when I called to tell him his marijuana plants were ready to be picked up that his dog was going to be at the animal hospital that night; so I took that as a good sign. I had been wondering how I'd get past that beast. Of course, he would have let me in if I'd delivered his plants in person. But what fun would that be?"

"Fun?"

"You know what I mean."

"I'm afraid I do. Did your son know what you were doing?"

"No."

"Then how did you get him to go all the way to Phoenix to kill Prospero?"

"He didn't. I did."

"For what it's worth, I don't believe you. But it's a moot point. He's already paid for his crime and your punishment will not depend on whether you killed him or not."

"My son is innocent."

"Maybe he WAS, but he DID try to kill me."

"He was just protecting his mother."

"Really? So your saying he was there when you tried to kill me just to watch? Now THAT'S what I call a loyal son - the kind who would willingly drive all the way to Arizona to kill someone he didn't know."

"I TOLD you..."

"I know. Well, the bottom line is that you just might get some leniency from a jury that hears your admittedly sad story. Maybe even from me if you hadn't killed Tom. As far as I'm concerned, you can rot in prison for the rest of your life for that."

"What, no gas chamber."

"Unlike you, I don't believe in the death penalty.

53

Christmas Eve had arrived, and our little family - Marjorie, Nancy, Duane, and I were having a modest pre-Christmas dinner of corned beef hash and baked beans in anticipation of a lot of turkey and stuffing the next day. I reminisced about how I'd tried unsuccessfully to get Marjorie's attention since the 8th grade, while she only remembered me as the geeky kid who got pantsed on the field in full view of her field hockey team in the 12th grade.

This would be the last Christmas Duane would be spending so much time with us. It would be the last Christmas I would be Chief Constable of Oak Hill. And it was a special day for another reason: it was Nancy's first Christmas with us since we adopted her nearly a year earlier. And I had a special present I couldn't wait to give her.

"Well, at least you won't have to endure a trial like you did last year."

"Nope, Marjorie, Alice Linderman has confessed to everything and will likely spend the rest of her life in prison."

"It's kind of sad, though, don't you think? After what she witnessed them doing to her little brother."

"Look, Marjorie, Tom Whitney and Lionel Carmody had nothing to do with her brother's death. She killed Tom for purely selfish reasons. And she said killing Knobb was fun. And maybe Carmody, too"

"Maybe?"

"Yeah, Duane, maybe. I'm almost certain she killed Tom, and she does confess to it. But I'm not so sure about Carmody. I think it's just as likely that her son, Grover, did that one, using her .22. Not that it matters much, now, with Grover dead and gone. Even if we found proof that she didn't do it, she's still looking at life. Bottom line, I really don't care whether she killed Carmody or not. In fact, I m not one hundred percent sure she killed Strand and Knobb. Grover might have done those, too, with the .22, and she just decided to protect his memory by making up a false confession, but I doubt that very much. In any case, she DID try to kill me, so I'm all but certain she did all the killings, except Prospero's. I only wanted to find Tom's killer, and I did. But whether she personally killed one or five people, or even none, she most certainly conspired in all their deaths. OUCH!"

"Your butt still hurts, dear?" I nodded and grimaced.

"Hey, boss, why are you so sure she and not her son did Tom?"

"Because all the evidence in Tom's killing indicates he had no inkling he was in danger. He was shot at close range in the back of the head by someone he did not suspect. And the forensics on the glass around the hole in Tom's patio door indicate it was cut from the inside, not the outside like the others, and done after Tom was dead.

"Couldn't that have been Grover?"

"Possibly, Duane, but I knew Tom pretty well, and I can't picture him letting a stranger in the house, turning off his alarm system, and turning his back on him. His fiancé, Laura said the same thing. He was more careful than that. But that seemingly nice old lady could have fooled him. Besides, her confession had a lot of detail that it's likely only the killer knew - detail I doubt her son would have shared with her. I think what happened was that Tom had found out about Strand working at the flower shop and just went there to cover all bases. But he evidently mentioned something that led Missus Lindermann to think she was in jeopardy of being found out, so she decided she had to kill him to protect herself. And, like me, it never occurred to Tom that Missus Lindermann was anything other than a harmless little lady. But I eventually came to the conclusion that it couldn't have been anyone else."

"But honey, why did she wait all those years to kill these people?"

"My guess? she didn't know the whereabouts of any of them, so she was able to keep it bottled up inside. But she had an unhappy life. Her beloved brother killed, her parents' early death, ditto her husband. Way down deep, I think she connected all her unhappiness to Ronald's brutal death with her watching in fear. The way I see it is that she had absolutely nothing to do with drugs or that her son was into drug trafficking until this came up. If she had been, I think she would have become aware of Walter Knobb and Cory Matcher much sooner, because their records indicate they'd been at it for some time. And the records confiscated at Hume Lake indicate that the flower shop had been involved, probably just through her son, for quite some time. It just doesn't fit anything we know about her that she was aware of it. But one day, in walks Walter Knobb, her son's partner in crime, and she recognizes him right away, at least by his name. That's when all her guilt and hatred kicked in and she began plotting to kill him. Then, when Knobb referred to Violet Strand also living in the next town, she decided to go all out for revenge. I think she not only wanted to kill them, but to make them pay in Hell. So she got her son to take that old photo she tore out of the Kodak album and had him go get four copies made at the Fotomat. That gave her five photos she could leave at the scenes in a way that would mean something to the souls of her victims, but nothing to the cops. And if Bud hadn't noticed the photos being identical, she might have succeeded. The clincher was when Harry and Bud found the remaining two photos at her home after she was arrested, as well as the bedroom window she practiced on to learn how to cut a hole in glass. In fact, I'm convinced that, had she not left those photos, she never would have been caught. There would have been no way in Hell...sorry Nancy, in Heck, that the motive for the murders would have ever been even guessed at much less revealed. And Missus Lindermann was incredibly meticulous about not leaving evidence, at least until she left tire tracks in the mud after Carmody's murder. And that was only because Irma and I showed up unexpectedly. Those tracks, too, have been linked to her son's car. So either she used his car, or he used her gun. Four photos: one for Walter, one for Violet, and one each for Gordon Prospero and Cory Matcher. And the one likely intended for Matcher was found in a dresser drawer. How she determined the whereabouts of Prospero is still a mystery. But I think that, when she realized that he lived so far away, in Phoenix, that she took her son into her confidence and got him to kill Gordon. She even gave him a copy of the photo, but she never gave him her .22. She probably thought there was no way Grover's .32 would ever be connected to the other murders so far away, or that the photo would mean anything to police there. And it didn't. But she was evidently so obsessed over needing to leave the photo for God to find that she took a chance that it could provide no clues to police here, either - her ONLY mistake. Incidentally, Phoenix is still considering trying her for his murder. I hope not.

"So they all paid for their youthful crime except for Cory Matcher."

"Maybe so, Duane, but my impression is that Cory has suffered many years of sleepless nights worrying about his soul over what he did. I'm pretty sure that if I'd done something like that at age thirteen, I never would have gotten over it. And by the way, this whole affair has brought him to the attention of the ATF, so he's not entirely off the hook as far as drug dealing is concerned.

54

On Christmas morning, we all got up early and sat around the tree. There were lots of presents. But the elephant in the room, so to speak, was a big present that was only haphazardly wrapped in three kinds of wrapping paper and a couple of colors of ribbons. We told Nancy it was hers.

When she tore off the wrapping and saw it was a Schwinn bicycle, she squealed with joy.

"I never had a bicycle before. Esau wouldn't let us have one."

"Well, at the ripe old age of eleven, it's time you did."

"But I don't even know how to ride one."

"Uncle Arnie and I will start teaching you today," said Duane, "and by tomorrow you'll be an expert."

"Arnie's not my uncle, he's my father."

I couldn't help it; I cried.

9 781796 038279